Casting Call

John Locke

TELEMACHUS PRESS

This book is a work of fiction. Names, characters, places and incidents are either the product of the author's imagination or are used fictitiously. Any resemblance to actual persons, living or dead, or to actual events or locales is entirely coincidental.

CASTING CALL

Cover Designed by: Telemachus Press, LLC
Copyright © iStockPhoto/000000053479
Copyright © iStockPhoto/000014341765

Published by: Telemachus Press, LLC
http://www.telemachuspress.com

Visit the author's website:
http://www.donovancreed.com

ISBN: 978-1-940745-58-9 (eBook)
ISBN: 978-1-940745-59-6 (Paperback)

Printed in the United States of America

10 9 8 7 6 5 4 3 2 1

The New York Times Best Selling Author
and
Amazon Kindle Million Club Author

John Locke has sold
more than 2,500,000 eBooks
...by word of mouth!

Thank you!

To learn more about John Locke,
visit his website:

http://www.DonovanCreed.com

John Locke

New York Times Best Selling Author
#1 Best Selling Author on Amazon Kindle

Donovan Creed Series:
Lethal People
Lethal Experiment
Saving Rachel
Now & Then
Wish List
A Girl Like You
Vegas Moon
The Love You Crave
Maybe
Callie's Last Dance
Because We Can!

Emmett Love Series:
Follow the Stone
Don't Poke the Bear!
Emmett & Gentry
Goodbye, Enorma

Dani Ripper Series:
Call Me!
Promise You Won't Tell?
Teacher, Teacher

Dr. Gideon Box Series:
Bad Doctor
Box
Outside the Box

Other:
Kill Jill
Casting Call

Young Adult:
A Kiss for Luck (Kindle Only)

Non-Fiction:
How I Sold 1 Million eBooks in 5 Months!

Casting Call

Prologue

MEGAN FRY IS sobbing.

She's on the floor, face down, hands tied behind her back. She has a hood over her head. Her nose and cheekbones are broken. She's gurgling blood. Her feet are on fire.

No, seriously. Her feet are on *fire!*

She can *smell* her flesh burning.

The man she can't see wanted $10 million wired to an offshore account. The money wasn't a problem. She has that much and more. She agreed to pay it, and made the necessary arrangements by phone as he pointed a loaded gun two inches from her left eye.

Now, long after his demands have been met, the torture continues.

She begs him to stop, offers to pay more. Offers sex. Offers anything he wants, but the torture continues.

Hours later she whispers, "If you won't stop, will you at least kill me? Please?"

He says, "Sorry."

"I'm ready to die. I want...to die."

"I know."

"If you won't kill me," she whimpers, "will you at least tell me what you *want?*"

"I want to torture you," he says, simply.

And so it continues, hour after hour, for no other reason than he enjoys hurting her.

Chapter 1

Monday.
Nashville, Tennessee.
Riverfront Park Music Festival.

"OMIGOD!" KAYLEE SAYS, pointing at the two men pissing on the guy passed out on the grass.

"The poor man!" Ivy says. "We need to *do* something."

"Are you *crazy?*"

"What if it was *you?*" Ivy says.

"There are 50,000 people here. Let someone else handle it."

Ivy sets her jaw. "Those 50,000 *had* their chance."

She takes off at a sprint.

Kaylee sighs, slowly works her way toward the scene, arrives in time to see Ivy screaming at the group of drunks who have circled the pissers, cheering them on.

"You should be *ashamed* of yourselves!" Ivy yells. "You're like children on a playground, egging on a fight! And *you!*" she says, pointing at the pissers. "What's *wrong* with you? Where's your *compassion?*"

The pissers stand there a moment, dicks in hand, unsure how to react. Like the drunks around them, they haven't made the decision to let this bossy 20-year-old end their fun so abruptly. But when Ivy drops to her knees beside the passed-out drunken man and attempts to revive him, they slowly disburse.

"Can you hear me?" she says leaning down to his ear.

Kaylee approaches with trepidation. "We should get him some medical help."

"That should be our last resort."

"Why?"

"They'll lock him up for the night."

"That's a good thing, isn't it?"

Ivy turns to her friend and frowns. "How would *you* like to wake up in the middle of the night in jail?"

Kaylee frowns, spreads her hands. "Where are you going with all this?"

"What do you mean?"

"How far are you planning to take it?"

Ivy looks at the man. He's about 30, relatively clean-cut, drunker than hell. His shirt's missing, and the back of his pants have been pulled down far enough to show the top half of his ass. His torso's covered with numerous shades of lipstick graffiti consisting of vulgar language and a drawing of a toilet bowl on his stomach. When Ivy first sighted the pissers they were aiming their streams at the toilet bowl pic, but by the time she got there they changed their minds and decided it would be more fun to soak his face and hair.

"We need to find out where he lives and take him home," she says.

"Not in my car," Kaylee says.

"A cab?"

"No cabbie would take him. He's drenched, reeking of piss."

"Maybe he drove here."

"Are you planning to dig through his pockets for his keys?"

"If I have to, yes. Can you do me a favor?"

"Not if it involves taking a single step closer."

"It doesn't. Can you buy me several bottles of water? I want to wash the urine off before trying to move him."

Kaylee sighs, then makes the long trek to the concession stand and waits in line 15 minutes to get 6 bottles of water, which she places in her tote bag. When she returns she's stunned to see the man sitting up, conversing with her friend. Kaylee removes the water bottles from her bag and says, "These were $4 each. You owe me $24."

"Thanks, Kaylee. This is Bobby Tang. As you can see, he's not drunk."

"I can't see that at all," Kaylee says. "He looks plastered."

"I think I was...drugged," Bobby says, thickly. "Your friend's...a...saint."

"You hear that?" Ivy says. "I'm a saint!"

"I believe he said you're insane. And I agree."

3

She and Ivy pour four of the waters over his head and chest; then Ivy helps him to his feet and pours the other two over his pants and shoes.

"He's got a car here somewhere," Ivy says. "I'm gonna drive him home."

"You're joking."

"He can't very well drive himself."

"Tell me again why this is *our* responsibility?"

"Because we're nice people."

Chapter 2

IT TAKES 40 paper towels from the ladies' room to blot Bobby Tang's pants and shoes enough to keep them from squishing when he walks. With Ivy's help, Bobby makes it to the parking lot, where his car, a BMW 5 GT, instantly upgrades his looks from decent to handsome. They climb in and she asks if he's okay.

"Much better now, thanks."

She fires up the engine, starts driving.

Time and the walk have had a positive effect on his condition, and by the time they hit the Interstate he's conversing normally, without pausing between words.

"You're staring at my face," he says. "Is there still some lipstick on my forehead?"

"No, you got most of it. I was just thinking you don't look Asian."

"Neither do you."

"Why would I look Asian?"

5

"Why would *I?*"

"Your name's Tang, right? Isn't that Asian?"

He laughs. "It's my stepfather's name."

"He's Asian?"

"Was."

"He changed ethnicity?"

"He died."

"Oh. Sorry."

"It's okay. That was years ago."

Their conversation begins with questions from Ivy and answers from Bobby, but quickly evolves to mutual interests. She finds him charming, he finds her cute. Their chat is only interrupted by his need to explain where to turn, or how long to stay on a particular street. She's driving slowly, so Kaylee can follow closely in her car. Even so, the trip from Riverfront to his house takes less than 20 minutes.

If surprise number one was the car, surprise number two is Bobby's house. Ivy curb-appraises it at $750,000. She's no expert, so when they pull into the driveway and stop, she asks Bobby to wait in the car a minute, gets out, and climbs into Kaylee's car to ask her opinion.

"I have no idea," Kaylee says. "But this house screams married with children!"

"He's divorced. No kids."

"How'd he wind up with the house?"

"Who cares? By the way, don't freak."

"Why?"

"I'm gonna hang with him a while."

Kaylee arches an eyebrow. "You can't be serious! He could be an axe murderer, for all you know!"

"I'll get him settled, maybe make him some dinner. Don't worry; I'll check him out on the Internet before doing anything."

"Before doing what, exactly?"

Ivy smiles.

"Omigod! You are such a slut!"

Ivy laughs. "I'm just saying he's worth a closer look."

"Shit. I am so jealous right now."

"I know."

"Who drugged him? Did he say?"

"He's not sure. He drove to the concert to meet some friends, had a couple drinks, and passed out. He said he's not on any medication, so it's not that. At one point he was talking to a girl, so it's possible someone got jealous and slipped something in his drink."

"Sounds sketchy."

"I agree. But if someone drugged *you* at Music Fest your theories would be sketchy, too. Anyway, we've got his name, license plate, and we know where he lives. I think he's safe."

"What's all that writing about?"

"On his body? Just a bunch of drunk assholes having fun. He's really embarrassed about it. Can you blame him?"

Kaylee laughs. "I saw his ass, you know."

Ivy frowns. "Put that out of your mind, okay?"

"Why's he just sitting there in the car?"

"I asked him to wait while I sent you home."

"He invited you to stay?"

"Sort of. I mean, I basically invited myself. You know, to stay with him until I'm certain he's okay."

"Does he like you?"

"I hope so. I aim to find out."

Kaylee sighs. "Don't get hurt."

"I won't."

"Yes you will."

They both laugh.

Kaylee shows her a sly look. "Might there be an epic walk of shame tomorrow morning?"

"I won't rule it out."

"Well, as long as you're going in with your eyes open. But call me if things go bad or you need a ride."

"Will do. Thanks."

"You'd do the same for me. Quick question: if he's normal?"

"Yeah?"

"If he's normal, and you decide you don't want him, hook me up, okay?"

Ivy smiles. "You're already trying to steal my new boyfriend?"

"In the event you don't want him."

"See you tomorrow."

"Lucky."

Chapter 3

NOW, IN BOBBY'S house, Ivy snoops while waiting for Bobby to finish his shower. She has no desire to invade his privacy beyond making sure his story adds up. In other words, if his "ex-wife's" panty drawer is full, maybe she's his *current* wife, visiting relatives out of town.

A quick search reveals no women's clothes in the bedroom closets. No panties or bras in the dresser drawers. She sneaks upstairs, checks the guest bedrooms for signs of a female in residence, and comes up empty. Last stop is the laundry room, where she finds no women's clothing in the washer and dryer.

Perfect!

But he's bound to be dating, right? So she'll want to know if any girlfriends have been sleeping over recently. She'll need a mere 10 seconds in the master bathroom to make that determination, and she's already formulated a plan to gain entry. In the meantime, she checks the search engines on her cell phone to see what the Internet has to say about her prospective boyfriend, Bobby Tang.

Very little, it appears, and nothing negative. For that, she's grateful.

It suddenly dawns on her the shower's been running an awfully long time. Wondering if Bobby might have passed out again, she rushes to the door, and knocks loudly.

She hears the water turn off.

"Sorry to interrupt," Ivy says, "but I was worried about you."

"I can't believe you're so nice! Thanks, I'm fine. I'm just having a problem getting all this lipstick off my back."

Ivy thinks: *Problem solved!*

"Wrap a towel around yourself and I'll give you a hand."

"Seriously?"

"You'd do it for *me*, wouldn't you?"

"Of course."

"Good." She waits a few seconds, then says, "Okay, I'm coming in."

Seeing Bobby with a towel around his waist gives her mixed emotions. The good news is he's fitter than she is.

That's also the bad news.

Ivy's not fat or chunky, but she's also not wafer thin, like most rich guys seem to prefer.

"Where do you keep your towels?" she says.

He points to a cabinet. She selects a facecloth, wets it under one of the sink faucets, squirts some hand soap on it.

"You're cute," Ivy says.

"Thanks. You are, too."

Ivy laughs. "Actually, I was reading one of the lipstick messages on your back."

"Oh." He shakes his head, laughs. "Awkward!" He pauses a moment, then says, "Is that all it says? That I'm cute?"

"Nope. The entire message is 'You're cute. Call me.' And there's a phone number."

"Seriously? Did she leave her name?"

"Bradley."

He laughs.

"Want me to copy down his number?"

"What would you do if I said yes?"

"Cry, probably."

"In that case, please remove it with all due speed."

"Poor Bradley," she says.

"Are there any other messages I couldn't reach?"

"There's one that says you're a human toilet."

"Let's keep that one," he says.

"Really?"

He laughs. "No, crazy girl! I'm joking!"

Ivy laughs. Then asks if he managed to get the letters BWC off his butt.

"I think so."

"I better make sure," she says, pulling his towel to the floor.

Five minutes later they're in Bobby's bed, fucking like it's the cure for cancer. Just before he comes, she says, "Not to kill the mood, but I'm not on the pill."

"Morning after?"

"Sorry."

"Okay. No problem."

He finishes outside her, and they hang out till he's ready for round two. Then three. At some point he either passes out or falls asleep. Next morning he wakes up, completely naked, with his wrists handcuffed to the bed posts.

"Ivy?" he says.

He looks around the room; then yells for her, in case she's in the bathroom.

No response.

"C'mon, Ivy! I need to pee!"

A few minutes later he yells, "If this is a joke, it's not funny!"

Later still: "Ivy, I'm *serious!*"

Then: "I'm *warning* you!"

And finally: "You fucking *bitch!*"

Chapter 4

Tuesday Morning.

FROM TIME TO time Bobby hears his cell phone buzzing on the night stand, but two hours pass before he hears someone moving about the house.

Shit!

The last thing on earth he wants to do is let his new housekeeper catch him naked, handcuffed to his bed.

Wait. That's second-to-last. The last thing he wants is to piss himself and ruin his mattress. Bobby's on the verge of doing just that when he hears the doorbell ring. A minute later his housekeeper taps on his bedroom door.

"Bobby?" she says.

"Please don't come in, Kennon. I'm not dressed."

"There's a Mr. Andrew Witt here to see you."

"He came *here?*"

"He said he's been trying to call your cell phone but you never picked up. He says it's important."

Bobby thinks a minute. "Tell him to come to my room, but please don't escort him here."

She pauses. "Is everything all right?"

"Everything's fine. I know it doesn't make any sense, but please humor me."

"Have I done something wrong?"

"No, of course not. I just—I really can't explain right now."

She hesitates a moment, then says, "I'll send him on back."

"Thanks, Kennon."

When Mr. Witt knocks on the door, Bobby says, "Please come in and close the door behind you."

Mr. Witt opens the door and does a double-take.

"Please," Bobby says.

"*Excuse* me?"

"The door?"

Mr. Witt closes it and says, "I think you've misunderstood my purpose for being here."

"Don't be ridiculous. Get these things off me, will you?"

"That's not part of the deal."

"What are you talking about?"

"We're not allowed to get involved, or influence the action in any way." He places his briefcase on the bed, opens it. Pulls out a folder and says, "I was studying your questionnaire last night, and nowhere did I find any references to your being gay, with a bondage fetish. We certainly don't object to casting gays or lesbians, it's just that we expect our reality stars to be completely forthcoming."

"Relax. *She* did it."

"Your *housekeeper?*"

"No. The girl. The one who spent the night."

"How'd she manage that?"

"Fuck if *I* know. Wait. She gave me X."

"Ecstasy? You're sure about that?"

"No. But that's what she claimed it was."

Mr. Witt frowns.

Bobby says, "Look. I know you're not supposed to get involved, but my bladder's about to burst. I'm about to piss my bed."

"May I sit on the edge of your bed?"

"Fine. But if you're not gonna help me, please don't stare."

"Not much to look at, is there?"

Bobby frowns. "If our roles were reversed, I'd set *you* free."

"Perhaps you don't value your job as much as I do."

"Please. This isn't just humiliating, it's dangerous."

Mr. Witt removes a pad and pen from his briefcase and starts writing. Then looks up and says, "Oh, very well. Where's the key?"

Bobby turns his head to search the room. "I have no idea. Can you check the floor?"

Mr. Witt gets to his feet, looks around the room. "I see no key. Maybe it's in the bed."

Bobby lifts himself up, then says, "Aw shit. You're not gonna believe this."

"What now?"

"She put it in my ass."

"In that case you're screwed, Mr. Tang. And I'm getting the distinct impression the girl from last night had nothing to do with this. Tell the truth: you put it there."

"No way! I swear!"

Mr. Witt sits back down, picks up his pen, resumes taking notes. After a moment he says, "Tell me about your housekeeper."

"If I do will you set me free?"

"Let's see how you do with the questions first."

"I'll answer anything you want if I can take a quick piss."

"Go ahead."

"Funny."

Mr. Witt looks at his pad. "Your housekeeper is one of the most beautiful young women I've ever seen. What's her name?"

"Kennon Tate."

"Age?"

"Twenty-two, I think."

"If you're fucking her, my life's a shit sandwich."

"I'm not. I've never touched her."

"You prefer men?"

"You know I don't."

"I'm trying to believe you, but you're giving me so little to go on."

"Kennon's already got a man in her life. An older, wealthy guy."

"You know that for a fact?"

"It's what she told me. Why? You don't believe her?"

"Let me put it this way: if you were an older, wealthy guy and Kennon was your girlfriend would you let her work as a housekeeper for a 31-year-old divorced man?"

"No fucking way."

"Maybe her boyfriend gets off on the idea. If I were you, I'd put the moves on her."

"She's not that type of girl. She's very shy. Religious, I think."

Mr. Witt chews on that a minute, then says, "Okay, let's see if I can award some points. You pretended to be passed out and remained in character most of the afternoon."

"I did. And people pissed on me."

"True. They also wrote vulgar comments and drew lewd pictures on your body."

"You saw that?"

"Certain portions of your ordeal were recorded."

Bobby perks up. "Can you use that footage for the show?"

"No. We've been through this before. We film enough to verify you completed the task, but we do it with cell phones, or hidden cameras. When the actual show goes into production we'll hire real actors and recreate the scenes with proper lighting and equipment. You've heard this several times, right?"

"I was just hoping to get an acting credit."

"You're labor, not talent," Mr. Witt says. Then adds, "Though you're awfully well-paid for these challenges."

"It's not all roses. Someone pulled my pants down and wrote BWC on my ass."

"Obviously a reference to the recent urban terrorist attacks."

"Whatever. And some bastard talked his girlfriend into sticking her finger in my ass."

"Really?"

"You didn't catch it on film?"

"No. And I'm a bit skeptical about some of these claims."

"Like what?"

"You claim she handcuffed you?"

"That's right."

"Where'd she get the handcuffs? Were they in her purse? Sorry, security checks purses at the Music Fest entrance. They'd never allow her to bring handcuffs into the concert area."

"They're *my* handcuffs."

Mr. Witt stares at him. "That's interesting. Go on."

"It's not that big a deal. After we did the X, things got hot and heavy. At some point she said I could tie her up if I wanted, so I told her about the handcuffs I keep in the closet."

"You claim not to have a bondage fetish."

"Not as far as *me* being handcuffed. But sure, I like to cuff the ladies."

"So you cuffed her. Then what happened?"

"I did things to her. Nothing creepy, just stuff she liked. Then I guess I passed out, and she handcuffed me."

"I'll need details regarding the specific acts you performed on her. But first tell me this: why do you think she left you handcuffed to the bed?"

"I have no fucking idea."

"Did you force her to do anal?"

"Of *course* not! Why would you even *think* that?"

"You have an obvious anal fixation. One girl sticks her finger in your ass, another shoves a key in there. What's next, I wonder?"

"Hopefully that's the end of it. And it's not a fixation, it's a fact."

"So you say. At any rate, I'm awarding you a full point for the performance you gave at the Music Fest."

"That's 10 grand, right?"

"That's correct. Was it worth it?"

"What do *you* think? I'm unemployed, with a mortgage."

Mr. Witt nods. "You also succeeded in getting a woman to come home with you under the worst possible circumstances."

"That's another point, right?"

"Getting her home wasn't part of the deal. Seducing her was the challenge. We would have accepted your car, a hotel room, a pasture, ditch, or even a dumpster."

"We did it here in my bed. Surely that counts."

"It would if we had proof. Did you video the sex?"

"No. But we sure as shit had sex."

Mr. Witt stares at his pad and prepares to write. "Tell me about the girl who brought you home. Start with her name."

"Ivy Allen."

"Age?"

"Nineteen, I think. Possibly twenty."

"You checked her ID?"

"I had no reason to doubt her."

"You're a braver man than me. Describe her hair."

"Short, light brown, blonde highlights."

"Body?"

"You should have all this on tape."

"Pretend we don't. It would be nice if what we have matches what you claim."

"I'm too pissed at her to be objective about her body."

"That's fine. I was trying to award you another point, but in the end it's your decision." He shifts his weight as if he's about to leave.

Bobby stops him, saying, "Wait. I performed the challenge. I deserve to be paid."

"Then give me details."

He closes his eyes a moment, conjuring the image. "Her body was good. A little soft, but nice."

"Breasts?"

"Two."

"Funny."

"What, you mean the size?"

"Start with that, if you like."

"Very small. I'd guess 32-A."

"And the nipples?"

"What do you mean?"

"Describe them. In precise detail."

"Is that really necessary?"

"We covered this throughout your orientation. Our depiction of these events has to be as honest and realistic as humanly possible. It goes to the very essence of the project.

We can't have someone showing up after the fact saying we fudged the details to build ratings. If her nipples were inverted, hairy, puffy, or oddly-shaped, we're not about to put a perfect-breasted woman in the scene. Think of it as a documentary, not a fiction piece."

"Her nipples were normal."

"No such thing. What color, pink?"

"More brownish. No hair around them."

"Did they harden to the touch?"

Bobby nods.

"How far did they protrude when erect?"

"I don't know. I didn't measure them."

"Were they the size of a pencil eraser?"

"That sounds about right."

"And the areolae?"

"About the size of a piece of pepperoni. Slightly darker than the nipple."

"What else?"

"She had small bumps."

"Around her nipples?"

"Yeah."

"Montgomery glands?"

"If you say so."

"Were the nipples pointed upwards, straight ahead, or downward?"

Bobby gives him a long look. "I think you might be insane."

"Why's that?"

"You really expect me to believe you're gonna find an actress who meets every one of these ridiculous parameters? You'd have to cast Ivy, and no one else."

"This is more for the book than the show."

"What book?"

Chapter 5

MR. WITT EXPLAINS the series of erotic books they've commissioned for the purpose of generating interest in the video production. Over the next 20 minutes Bobby experiences the most extreme bladder discomfort imaginable, but he soldiers on, answering the most detailed and personal questions imaginable with regard to Ivy's body. But after being repeatedly quizzed about her clitoral hood and the tightness of her vagina, he snaps.

"What are you trying to get me to say? That her pussy was so tight it could crack walnuts? That you couldn't pound a dime into it with a sledgehammer? That it's narrower than my chances of getting into heaven?"

"Absolutely! Assuming those comments are true."

"Look. I've told you all I can remember. Surely it's enough for the book."

"Could you tell if she'd ever been pregnant?"

"You mean did she have a C-Section scar?"

"Did she?"

"No."

"Any stretch marks on her boobs?"

"I don't think so."

Mr. Witt nibbles on his bottom lip a minute. Then says, "The young lady you've described sounds like a natural."

"At what?"

"Breastfeeding."

"Come again?"

"Never mind. I'll move this along. On a scale from one to ten, how would you rate her overall looks?"

Bobby says, "That's subjective."

"How so?"

"I wouldn't have cast that guy who stars in Boardwalk Empire."

"Who, Steve Buscemi?"

"Yeah. I mean, not in the lead role."

"Because of his looks?"

Bobby nods.

Mr. Witt says, "I get that. But we're talking about women. So let's use a test case. We've both seen your house-keeper, Kennon. How would you rate her?"

"A ten. Easily."

"I agree. So on that basis, what's Ivy?"

"A solid eight."

"You're saying she's prettier than 80% of the women her age throughout the country?"

"Yeah. That's exactly where I'd put her. Top 20%."

"And her voice?"

"Her voice? What about it?"

"Whatever you can remember."

"Are you serious?"

"It's important."

Bobby sighs.

By the time Mr. Witt finishes chronicling every last detail including the length, shape, and color of Ivy's toenails, Bobby can't focus on anything beyond his bursting bladder. Tears are welling in his eyes.

"If you don't stop, I'll die," he says.

"Just wet the bed."

"Unacceptable."

"Suit yourself. In any event, I've got what I need. Congratulations."

"For what?"

"I'm awarding you a second point. That's 20 grand."

"Thank God!"

Mr. Witt removes a small device from his briefcase.

"What's that?" Bobby says.

"A miniature video cam."

"What's it for?"

"I'm going to give you the opportunity to add a quarter point."

"Another twenty-five hundred?"

"That's right."

"What do I have to do?"

"Talk Kennon into setting you free."

"What? That's crazy! She'll never do it. She'll freak out."

"Your challenge will be to convince her."

"She's going to think *you* handcuffed me!"

Mr. Witt smiles. "It's perfect. You see that, don't you? It adds a whole new component to the scene. This is what I love about my job! Every challenge creates an unexpected dividend."

"I should get a full point for this. It's particularly humiliating."

Mr. Witt puts the questionnaire, pad, and pen back in his briefcase, and shuts it, then stands up and scours the room for an unobtrusive spot to place the camera. When he finds one, he programs the signal into his cell phone.

"You're going to video it?"

"I am. Congratulations, Mr. Tang. You've earned a lot of money in a short period of time."

He starts to leave.

"Wait!" Bobby says. "When do I get paid?"

"If you're done, I'll have them send it to you today. If you want to earn more, there are some other challenges you can attempt."

"Can I do both? Get paid today for what I've done and keep performing challenges? I wouldn't ask, except I'm already two payments behind on my house and car."

"Tell you what. If you can get Kennon to set you free, I'll make it happen."

"Can you at least remove the key from my ass so she won't have to do it?"

"Don't be silly. That's the most compelling part of this challenge."

Bobby frowns. "If she runs out of here screaming, will you at least come back with bolt cutters?"

"Let's see how it turns out."

"You wouldn't let me die like this, would you?"

"Don't be so dramatic. I'll tell Kennon you'd like to speak to her."

Chapter 6

KENNON TAPS ON Bobby's door tentatively. She says, "Mr. Witt told me to check on you. He said it's urgent."

Bobby takes a deep breath. "He's right. It is."

"What's wrong?"

"I've got a bit of a situation."

"What's happened?"

"I need your help. Please try not to scream when you come in the door."

"Are you okay? You're frightening me!"

"I know. And I'm sorry. Just so you know, Mr. Witt refused to help me, which means you're my only hope."

"For what?"

"I had a date last night. Things got a little out-of-hand."

"What are you saying? You *killed* her?"

"No, of course not!"

"I'm coming in."

"Wait! I need to—"

Bobby was about to say he needed to explain the situation first, but it's too late. Kennon's in the room. As predicted, she screams. Then surprises him, saying, "You poor man!"

"Huh?"

She covers her eyes with a hand. "How long have you been like this?"

"Hours."

"This is the result of a *date*?"

"A date gone bad. She left me like this. Guess she thought it was funny."

"She should be *horsewhipped*! And *you* should have said something when I first arrived."

"I was too embarrassed."

"And Mr. Witt refused to help?"

"He thought it would be funny if you had to set me free."

"Why?"

"Because he knew it would be terribly embarrassing for me."

"What sort of man would treat a friend like that?"

"Mr. Witt and I are not friends. He's helping me find work."

Kennon pauses, as if trying to decide what to do with that information. Finally, she says, "Will he be stopping by the house regularly?"

"I don't think so. Why do you ask?"

"I don't particularly care for him."

"Because he left me handcuffed?"

"Not only that, but he forced me to rescue you."

"I'm truly sorry about that."

"Even if he thought it was funny, he should have at least covered you up. It shows a complete lack of respect for my dignity."

"I agree. I'm sorry."

"But apart from all that, he's creepy."

Bobby frowns. "Did he say something to you?"

"He asked if I'd ever nursed a child."

"*What?*"

She shrugs.

Bobby's eyes instinctively go to her chest, and remain there. Can't get caught staring if she's refusing to look at him, right? He continues staring while saying, "I don't know Mr. Witt that well, but I'm sorry he made you uncomfortable."

"It's okay," she says. "I'll fetch you a towel."

She disappears into the master bath, comes back a moment later holding a large, white towel. Then bites her lip and says, "I'm not staring, I promise."

"It's okay."

But it's *not* okay, because Bobby's been staring at *her*. His eyes were all over Kennon's chest a moment ago, then on her ass when she left the room to fetch the towel. Yes, she's beautiful, and yes, he's naked, and yes, the whole situation is crazy, but he didn't expect his body to react *this* way. Under normal circumstances, Bobby's penis length and girth is average at best.

But not today.

He looks down and can't believe what he sees. This is a *raging* hard-on, the mother of all erections. He's chubbed like Roman Polanski at a Girl Scout jamboree.

As Kennon attempts to drape the towel over his penis, she catches a glimpse and shouts, "Oh! Omigod! *Stop* it!"

"*Stop* it?"

"You know what I mean."

"It's a natural reaction to your beauty."

"There's nothing natural about *that*. It's—"

"What?"

"It's *purple!*"

"Just the head."

She frowns. "If that thing erupts, you could lose an eye."

"You're being silly."

"If I find out you've staged this whole thing..."

"I didn't. I swear."

She throws the towel at his crotch, but misses the target. To put it more accurately, the towel has encircled the base of his manhood without actually covering the vertical portion. Picture a bathroom plunger. While averting her eyes, Kennon tries to grab the towel with her thumb and index finger, but her fingernail spears one of his balls, causing him to yelp in pain.

"Sorry!" she says.

"It's okay. My fault completely."

"I'm only succeeding in making matters worse. In order to properly cover you up I'm afraid I'll have to look."

"It's okay. You made every effort not to."

"Yes. So anyway, here goes." Kennon drapes the towel over his engorged penis the same way Bobby used to drape the giant dust cover over his fake Christmas tree each year. Then she says, "Where's the key?"

Bobby rolls onto his side, which causes the towel to fall away.

"She gives him a stern look. You did that on purpose!"

"I didn't intend for the towel to come off, but yeah, I purposely rolled onto my side."

"Is this some sort of sick joke? How can you possibly think I want to see your ass?"

"That's where the young lady placed the key after hand-cuffing me."

"*What? Where?*" Then it hits her. "Omigod! Surely you don't expect me to...."

"You're my only hope."

"I may have to re-think my employment."

"I was passed out. Ivy, the young lady who did this—"

"Why would you allow that type of woman into your bedroom?"

"I haven't been with a woman in a long time. I'd been drinking. She drove me home. It's...a long story."

Kennon looks at his backside and frowns. "How deep is it in there?"

Bobby feels like saying, *my ass or the key?* But settles for: "I'm not sure."

"Are you in pain?"

"Not from the key, but I'm desperate to pee. Please do what you can."

Kennon scowls deeply, then leans over his bed and replaces the towel. Then says, "I'll try not to hurt you." She leans over, spreads his ass cheeks, gets her fingers around the key, and retches. She extracts the key, drops it on the bed, sprints to the toilet, vomits.

Bobby sighs, looks at the key on the bed, and waits for her to return.

Chapter 7

Marriott Hotel.
Bowling Green, Kentucky.
One Month Earlier.

TOMMY BUMPUS ENTERS the hotel meeting room with tight jeans and the confidence of a state fair cookware salesman. But when he realizes the room is completely empty except for Mr. Witt, and a tabletop video cam and speaker, he balks. A voice from the speaker says, "Name?"

The voice is purposely distorted, but female.

"Well, hey there, Sugar!" he says. I never spoke to a video cam before, but since you're a woman, what you really need to know about me is right here!"

He lifts his t-shirt, shows his six-pack. He's early 20's with sandy hair and a gym rat's body. He adds, "How you like that, sweetheart?"

"Name?" she repeats with a complete lack of emotion.

"Stick Shift."

She says nothing.

He quickly adds, "My given name's Tommy Bumpus, but folks around here call me Stick Shift. It's my handle." He shows her his best practiced smile.

"Who?"

"Ma'am?"

"Who calls you Stick Shift?"

He winks. "The ladies."

"I'm a lady. I see no reason to call you that."

He flashes a sly grin. "It's on account of my *package*. If you were to see it, you'd understand. Trust me on that, darlin'."

"Show me."

"Huh?"

"Show me your package."

He laughs. "I can't do that! You're filmin' me!"

"You want this job?"

"Well, sure. I mean, I think so. Don't know what it's about yet, but sure."

"Then show me your package."

"Here?"

"That's right."

"You mean right now?"

"Mr. Bumpus, I'm a casting director. I'm accepting one application per city, at most. You're in this room because you passed the preliminary. Either pull your pants down or walk away."

"But....Why?"

"You were told in the pre-interview we require 100% honesty from our reality candidates. *Knowing* this, you waltzed into my interview cockier than Barney Fife with a new pistol grip, saying your package is a huge selling feature with the ladies. You also said I'd understand if I saw it. So let's see it."

Tommy's face shows concern.

She says, "Never mind. Thanks for your time. Next?"

"Wait!" he says.

He reluctantly pulls his pants down to his knees.

"I see underwear," she says. "No stick shift."

He sighs, slides his underwear down.

She's silent a moment. "That's it?"

"I wasn't ready."

"I'll wait."

He pulls on it a moment.

She says, "Is it supposed to get smaller when you rub it? Because that's what seems to be happening."

Frustrated, Tommy says, "Look. This never happened before, okay? Maybe if you were here in person, I'd be able to—"

"Maybe if you turned sideways," she says.

He does.

She says, "I'm still not impressed."

"I think maybe I need to pee first."

"Well, you'll have to pee somewhere else. Thank you. Next?"

"Ma'am?"

"We're done here, Mr. Bumpus." She says, "Mr. Witt? Are you still there?"

"I am."

"Please escort this one out and bring in the next one."

Tommy says, "Can I have another chance? You know, start over? Like this never happened?"

"No. But I won't rule you out on the basis of this interview alone."

"Thank you!"

"But if we *do* choose to hire you I'll insist you change your nickname."

"To what?"

"Cigarette Lighter. Good day."

Mr. Witt escorts Tommy out, then brings in the next candidate.

The voice on speaker says, "Your name?"

"Bobby Tang."

"Where are you from, Bobby?"

"Nashville."

"As you were told in the pre-interview, we're selecting one person only from this location. Why should it be you?"

"I lost my job, my wife left me, and I just cashed my last unemployment check."

"In other words, you're desperate."

"I am."

"I like desperate. Step closer to the camera."

Chapter 8

Nashville, Tennessee.
Present Day (Tuesday).
11:00 a.m.

MR. ANDREW WITT climbs two flights of steps, turns left, walks to the third apartment, knocks on the door.

He hears movement inside. The door opens as far as the chain allows. A young lady peers out and says, "Yes?"

"You must be the roommate."

"Excuse me?"

"Does Ivy Allen live here?"

"Who are *you*?"

"Andrew Witt."

"Who're you with, Mr. Witt?"

He passes his business card through the opening. She stares at it a moment, then says, "Just a minute."

Then she closes the door.

A full minute passes before Mr. Witt hears the chain sliding off the track. Sees the door open.

"Ivy?"

"Yes?"

"May I come in?"

"Yes, of course. I have to apologize for the mess."

"That's quite all right. I know you weren't expecting me."

He follows her into the small sitting room. "Can we have a short chat?"

Ivy calls out, "Kaylee? Can you give us some privacy?"

Kaylee enters the room and says, "You actually want me to leave the apartment?"

"If you don't mind."

She cocks her head at Mr. Witt and raises her eyebrows.

He blushes. "It's not like that."

"Like what?" Kaylee says.

"We'll only be a few minutes," Ivy says.

"Fine." She grabs her cell phone from the kitchen, exits the apartment, walks down the stairs, waits in the courtyard.

Ivy removes the clothes from the chair closest to Mr. Witt and deposits them on the corner of the couch. Then clears a space for herself on the middle of the couch, and sits.

Mr. Witt places his briefcase on his knees, opens it, removes the pad and pen, closes the case, and uses it as a makeshift desk.

He starts writing. After a moment he looks up and says, "Yesterday afternoon you attended the Music Fest."

She nods.

"You saw a man lying on the ground, covered in writing."

"Bobby Tang."

Mr. Witt writes the name down. Then says, "Was he drunk?"

"No, but he'd been drugged."

"You helped him to his feet?"

"Yes. Some horrible men had urinated all over him. It was so gross. I washed the urine off with bottled water."

"What happened next?"

She tells him every detail of her encounter with Bobby, leaving nothing out. When she finishes her story he says, "Do you have any proof?"

She shows him several photos of Bobby, passed out, naked, handcuffed to his bed.

He says, "Can I send these to my email?"

"If you'd like."

They're quiet till Mr. Witt says, "Ivy, I'm going to give you a full point for seducing Bobby Tang last night."

"Omigod! Ten thousand *dollars*? *Thank* you!"

"My pleasure. And I'm giving you another quarter point for handcuffing him."

She grins. "I wasn't sure if you'd accept that. You said to look for a man lying on the ground with writing all over him, and if I could seduce him I should try to tape or tie him, but when I heard he owned some handcuffs I figured—"

He cuts her off in mid-sentence with a wave of his hand. "The cuffs were brilliant, Ivy! And sticking the key up his ass? A stroke of genius! That's a wonderful example of improvisation, exactly the sort of thing we encourage when it comes to our reality stars. We never anticipated that, and therefore I'm awarding you another quarter point."

"*Seriously?*"

"That's $15,000."

"I can't *believe* it!"

"I just have one question for you."

"What's that?"

"Why did you leave without saying goodbye?"

"I knew he'd be angry. I didn't want to get yelled at."

"Because you like him?"

She bites her lip. "No. I mean, at first I thought I might, but he's not quite what I was hoping for."

"Can you explain your feelings?"

"He seemed like the perfect catch, but then I found out he's still married, loves his wife, and he's broke."

"How'd you find that out?"

"He told me."

"When?"

"After we had sex."

"The first time?"

"Third."

"You said earlier you fucked him three times. I didn't mention it at the time, but I'm impressed. You really worked hard for your money."

"I really wanted that quarter point for tying him up! But he wouldn't pass out, so I had to keep him busy."

"You took a huge chance letting *him* handcuff *you*. You didn't know the guy. He could have done something to you."

"Bobby's harmless. My biggest fear was he'd pass out before taking them off me."

"When did you drug him?"

"After the first encounter I made him a sandwich. After the second, I opened some wine."

"Which did you drug, the sandwich or the wine?"

"Both."

Mr. Witt nods. Then says, "So after the third sexual session he told you he was broke?"

"After the third session he started crying. The drugs probably had something to do with it. He said he loves his wife, and wants her to come back. I asked him why she left. He said he lost his job and couldn't pay the mortgage on his house and car." She pauses, then adds, "But you know what's weird?"

"Tell me."

"He has a housekeeper."

"He does?"

"Uh huh."

"How do you know? Was she there?"

"No, but the place was spotless. I told him I'd never seen such a clean house, and he said he had a housekeeper."

"How can he afford to pay her?"

"I asked him the same thing. He said his parents hired her."

"Do *they* have money?"

"I doubt it. If they did I expect he'd be current with his mortgage."

Mr. Witt nods slowly. Then says, "So the reason you felt comfortable leaving him handcuffed to his bed was—"

"His housekeeper. I figured she'd set him free."

"And if she doesn't show up at work today?"

"She did. I called. When she answered, I hung up."

"You're a caring person."

"Thanks. I mean, I wouldn't just leave him there all day." She pauses. "Do you have any other challenges for me?"

"Will you show me your panties?"

"Seriously?"

He nods.

She stands, pulls her warm up pants down to her knees. Turns a slow circle. "How's that?"

"Nice. Thanks." As she pulls her pants back up he adds, "Confucius once said, 'Panties not best thing in world but next to it.'"

"What's that mean?"

"Think about it."

She does, but gets nowhere, so she gives up and says, "How much do I get for that?"

"For what?"

"Showing you my panties."

"Nothing."

"What do you mean?"

"It wasn't a challenge. I was just asking."

Ivy frowns. "That was a dicky thing to do."

Mr. Witt smiles. "Agreed. But there's a lesson in it."

"What's the lesson? I shouldn't trust you?"

"The lesson is by acting impulsively you allowed me to press my advantage." Noting the confused look on her face he says, "No matter. To answer your question, yes. I do have something in mind for you."

She cocks her head, suspiciously.

He smiles. "Yes, this is an actual challenge, not a request. Something I'll pay you to do."

"What is it?"

"Something I'm working on. It will involve two women. You and someone else I'll have to recruit. I can let you know in a couple of hours."

"I've got another question."

"Ask it."

"What if Bobby watches the series and figures out you paid me to have sex with him?"

"Not to worry. Our payment to you won't be part of the script."

"Good," she says, relieved. Then laughs and says, "How funny would it be if you paid *him* to seduce *me*?"

Mr. Witt laughs. "That'd be hilarious! You have a fertile imagination, Ivy. We should have hired you as a script consultant!"

Chapter 9

KAYLEE WATCHES FROM the courtyard as Mr. Witt leaves the apartment and walks down the stairs. She allows two minutes for him to get to his car, then climbs the steps, opens the door, gives Ivy a hard stare and says, "I heard everything."

She points at the laptop on the far side of the couch. "I recorded you on my webcam."

Ivy frowns. "When?"

"I set it up right after he knocked on the door. I knew something was up. I knew you were gonna make me go outside."

"I can't believe you invaded my privacy."

"I can't believe you *played* me like that!"

"What are you *talking* about?"

"The seduction of Bobby Tang."

"What about it?"

"You acted like it was a chance encounter. Now I learn you planned the whole thing, and fucked him for money! Like a common whore."

"*Common* whore? Really, Kaylee? I just earned $15,000 for a one night stand with a guy who could have been the one."

"You should have told me what was happening."

"I wasn't *allowed* to tell anyone."

"I'm not *anyone*. I'm your best friend."

"Lucky me. My best friend just called me a common whore."

"That was me being pissed. Not that it changes things. You took money to fuck a stranger."

Ivy laughs derisively. "Two weeks ago we went to *Jump Red.*"

"So?"

"Before I was two sips into my drink you were blowing a paralegal in the parking lot."

"Omigod! You are such a bitch to say that!"

"True or false?"

"That wasn't my fault and you know it!"

"Not your fault?"

"He claimed he was a criminal lawyer. A partner in a famous law firm."

"Which means you blew him for money."

"That's bullshit. He didn't pay me a cent."

"Sorry to split hairs, but had he told the truth about his job, you wouldn't have blown him at all."

"So?"

"It's the same thing."

"It's not. I blew a cute guy, hoping for a relationship."

"A relationship that might offer you financial security."

"You can turn it any way you want, but the truth is you agreed to fuck a guy you never even met."

"That's not remotely true. I was offered a challenge. All I agreed to do was take a look at the guy. When I saw him at the park I wasn't sure. But after talking to him and cleaning him up I decided to drive him home. But I had you follow us to his house because I still wasn't sure. When we were in his driveway I told you the truth: after talking to him, I thought he was worth a closer look. But even then I wasn't positive I'd have sex with him. Before that happened I checked him out on the Internet and searched his house to verify he was divorced. I never agreed in advance to perform the challenge, and could have stopped at any time. If you compare my actions with Bobby to what you did with the paralegal at *Jump Red*, I think you'll agree I knew who I was fucking, and you didn't."

After a minute of silence, Ivy's features soften. She says, "Look. We both had sex with a stranger thinking he could be the guy. The real difference is I knew I had a chance to get some serious cash and be a part of a cable TV series. Now tell me you wouldn't have done the same thing."

Kaylee says, "I want in on it."

"It might be too late. They haven't screened you."

"You could vouch for me. Mr. Witt said he needed two girls for the next challenge. You could call him and tell him I'll do it."

"Are you sure?"

Kaylee nods. "You're not the only one who needs cash."

Ivy cocks an eyebrow. "What if the challenge involves having sex with a stranger?"

"I can overlook any morality concerns, since my roommate has already set the example."

Ivy gives her a smirk, but says, "I don't have his phone number, but he just sent some photos to his email account, so I've got that address. I'll see what I can do."

Chapter 10

Tuesday, 1:30 p.m.
Megan Fry.

IT'S BEEN A long six days for Megan.

She's been beaten, humiliated, tortured, and interrogated. The beating consisted of single full-force punches to the face or stomach. Punches she couldn't see because she was still wearing the hood. Punches that came at her soundlessly, without warning, from all angles, and hurt like hell.

The torture was different.

The man took his time, told her exactly what he was going to do, then did it. She knew by the explanations that certain tortures would induce maximum pain, but some were less obvious. For example, setting her feet on fire for 20 seconds at a time, then rinsing them with rubbing alcohol—was obvious.

But the chair torture was far worse.

That one seemed tame when he described it. After sleep-depriving her for two days and nights, he put a wooden chair on top of another wooden chair, placed the hood over her head, tied her hands behind her back, and placed her on the upper chair. As she drifted asleep, her shifting weight caused the chair to topple, and send her crashing to the concrete floor.

Over and over, hour after hour.

What made it so much worse than it sounds was the combination of mental and physical pain it involved in the space of two nightmarish seconds. The first second occurred when she'd wake up realizing she was falling and couldn't use her hands to break the fall. The next second was the sudden splat as her head, back, shoulders or face crashed into the floor, unprotected. It could never be predicted, nor prepared for, since every fall came from a different angle and struck a different part of her body full-force against the floor.

There was also a firecracker torture, where he placed a low-grade miniature firecracker between her toes, and lit an extremely long fuse. Some fuses detonated the tiny explosives, but most didn't. But the sound of each fuse burning created a sense of panic that lasted for several seconds, followed by total relief, or sudden, boiling pain as a small chunk of meat was blown from between her toes.

The anticipation was almost as bad as the explosion.

Another particularly nasty torture he employed was measured suffocation. The way he explained it, "As you start to suffocate, carbon dioxide builds in your body, generating higher pH levels. This triggers the fear response in the part of your brain that's wired for survival." She could tell he smiled before adding, "Trust me, it's far worse than it sounds. It's akin to the sensation prisoners experience during waterboarding sessions."

He was right. She experienced hours of chest pains from the panic he induced over several five-minute sessions.

The good news is he hasn't raped her yet, though he constantly threatens to sodomize her with a lighted Roman candle.

She'd like to avoid that particular horror, if at all possible.

Chapter 11

Same Day, Same Time.
Bobby Tang.

BOBBY NORMALLY LETS Kennon answer the doorbell, but on the chance it could be Mr. Witt, he'd rather not upset her again. In the hours since his handcuffing incident, she's been avoiding him like the plague. Bobby walks to the door, looks through the peephole, and see's the girl from last night. Not Ivy, but the other one.

He opens the door.

"Remember me?" she says.

"Your name's on the tip of my tongue, but I can't quite—"

"Kaylee."

"Kaylee! Right." He looks past her on the doorstep. "Where's Ivy?"

"Home, far as I know. Before you ask, no, she didn't send me. She has no idea I'm here, and I hope you won't tell her."

"Did she tell you what happened last night? What she did?"

"Yes and no."

"What's that mean?"

Kaylee says, "Can I come in?"

Bobby nods, and leads her to the den. When they realize Kennon has just entered the doorway, Kaylee whispers, "Can we talk privately?"

Bobby says, "It's fine, Kennon. I've got this."

Kennon takes a step into the room and says, "May I pour you some tea, Miss?"

Kaylee shakes her head, no.

Bobby says, "I think we're okay for now, Kennon. Thank you."

"Very well," Kennon says, stiffly. She pauses a moment before leaving the room.

Kaylee asks, "Is that your wife?"

"Housekeeper."

"Does Ivy know?"

"Why would Ivy know? Or care?"

"Well, I mean, she's breathtaking. Your housekeeper, I mean."

"Kennon."

"Yes. You must be paying her a ton."

"You'd think so, but that's not the case. Doesn't make sense, does it?"

Kaylee cocks her head. "I can guess what most people think."

"Tell me."

"That she performs services outside the normal definition of housekeeping."

He shakes his head and chuckles. "Not for me, she doesn't. Nor will she ever, after hearing what happened with Ivy last night."

"Did you notice she seemed overly concerned just now, about me being here? She didn't want to leave the room."

"She probably thinks you're Ivy. She's not a fan."

"You told Kennon about last night?"

"I had to. She's the one who set me free this morning. You're aware your friend left me handcuffed to the bed last night and shoved the key up my ass, right?"

Kaylee suppresses a smile. "I did happen to hear that."

"It's probably funnier to an outsider."

"Sorry. Still, having a beautiful girl like Kennon rescuing you..."

"What about it?"

"Well, I mean, that must have been fun." She gives him a wink. "For *you*, at least."

"Not as much as you'd think." He lets that comment sit for a minute, then says, "I've distracted you."

"From what?"

"Your reason for being here."

Kaylee smiles. "Sorry. I know whatever's going on with your housekeeper is none of my business. It's just that in my experience girls who look like that don't have to clean houses for a living."

"I'm sure it's temporary. She's probably going through a phase of some sort, or doing penance for some religious infraction. I didn't hire her, by the way, my parents did."

"Seriously? Wow! Would you consider trading parents with me?"

"I'll say no. So anyway, what brings you here?"

"I found out something."

"About what?"

"Ivy."

He steeples his hands, then opens his palms and says, "I'm listening."

"Do you like her?"

"Not as much as when I first met her. Why do you ask?"

Kaylee takes a deep breath. "Can this be our little secret?"

"If you like."

"I'd have to insist."

"Okay. Whatever you tell me will stay between us. I promise."

She searches Bobby's face a moment, then says, "An hour ago a man named Andrew Witt showed up at our apartment to have a long talk with Ivy."

It isn't easy, but Bobby forces his expression to remain neutral.

Kaylee says, "Do you know Mr. Witt?"

"I don't think so," Bobby lies.

Kaylee says, "I'm not trying to get into your business, Bobby. It's just that if this had happened to me, I'd want someone to tell me."

"What are we talking about, exactly?"

"This man, Mr. Witt paid Ivy $10,000 to have sex with you last night."

Bobby's eyes go large. "She's a *hooker?*"

"No. She's doing challenges for some sort of cable TV show."

Bobby's face turns whorehouse red.

Kaylee says, "You needn't be embarrassed. Ivy's not a hooker, and this wasn't just about the money. At the time she seduced you she thought you might be the one."

Bobby considers her words carefully, then rejects them. "She took the money, though, didn't she?"

"She did."

"And you're telling me all this because?"

"I think you're a good guy. I like you."

"I don't understand."

"Yesterday, at the park, Ivy made the first move to help you. I hung back, not wanting to get involved. Of course, at the time I didn't know she was being paid to help you. But after we cleaned you up, I realized you were normal."

"Normal how?"

"You turned out not to be a drunk. Anyway, Ivy made the first connection with you, so I held back, like any good friend would do. And had it turned out that Ivy wanted to date you, I wouldn't have shown up on your doorstep today."

"She decided I'm not the one?"

"Right."

"And has no interest in dating me?"

"That's correct."

"Why not?"

"She thinks you're broke, and still hung up on your wife."

"But suddenly *you're* interested in dating me?"

Kaylee blushes. "Yes."

She lowers her eyes in case Bobby wants to give her body a closer look through the filter of this new information. If he does, she figures to match up pretty well against her roommate. While Ivy's slightly prettier, she's also chubby, with smaller boobs. Taking all things into consideration, they're pretty equal. Kaylee brings her gaze back up to Bobby's face and is pleased to see his eyes lingering on her boobs.

"See something you like?" she asks, playfully.

"Huh?"

She smiles. "Bobby, I think you're totally hot. I liked you the moment I heard you explain what happened yesterday. I was quite jealous when Ivy took you inside. This morning I asked her a million questions, and decided you've got high relationship potential."

"What are you saying?"

"I may not be as pretty as Ivy, but I might be a better match for you."

"In what way?"

"One, I don't care about your financial condition. Two, I'm not threatened by your feelings toward your wife. And three, I'm nicer, less bitchy, and more passionate than Ivy. I'm positive I could hold your interest and keep you happy."

Bobby takes a deep breath, lets it out slowly. "Look. Don't take this the wrong way, but—"

Kaylee's face falls. "Shit."

"What?"

"Omigod!"

Kaylee stands, turns to leave.

Bobby says, "What's wrong?"

She turns back. "I'm such an idiot. I threw myself at your feet and you don't even find me attractive." She closes her eyes, humiliated. Shakes her head. "I can't tell you how embarrassing this is." She opens her eyes, says, "It's not your fault. I know I came across totally desperate just now. That's not me. Not normally, anyway. I think it's just—I've got so much to give a man, and never seem to find a good one. Or at least, one who thinks I'm a catch, and—"

Bobby puts his hand up to stop her. "It's not that."

"Of course it is."

"Please sit."

She shakes her head. "I can't. I'm about to cry. You don't want to see that."

"Please," Bobby says. "I think you look great. Very sexy. Better than Ivy."

She studies his face, and very reluctantly, sits. But in the chair, not the couch where she'd been sitting.

Bobby says, "Please hear me out. A moment ago you didn't give me a chance to finish my sentence. I was about to say don't take this the wrong way, but did Mr. Witt pay you to seduce me?"

"*Excuse me?*"

"I don't know this Mr. Witt character, but I'm beginning to think he must have had something to do with me getting drugged at the park yesterday. I haven't had a date in the two months since my wife left, but suddenly *two* beautiful women are interested in me? You said he paid Ivy to seduce me for some sort of TV reality show, and now *you're* interested in a relationship? Is it just me, or does this sound suspicious? No offense."

"You think I'm beautiful?"

"What?"

"A moment ago you said, 'two beautiful women.' You were referring to me and Ivy."

"Well, you *are* beautiful."

She shows him a demure smile and says, "The short answer is no, Mr. Witt hasn't paid me to seduce you, and I can prove it."

"How?"

"By telling you the job Mr. Witt is gonna offer you."

"*Me?* I've never met the man!"

"Not yet, maybe, but you *will*."

"How can you be so sure?"

"I eavesdropped on him and Ivy. Want to know what they said?"

He nods.

Kaylee bites her lip, starts to speak. But before the words come out, Bobby's cell phone rings. Caller ID says it's Mr. Witt.

Bobby puts his finger to his lips, then takes the call.

Chapter 12

"HELLO?"

"You've lost your mojo, Bobby."

"Excuse me?"

"I've been thinking it over," Mr. Witt says, "replaying it in my mind."

"What's that, Mr. *Witt?*" Bobby says, winking at Kaylee.

She grins and mouths the words, *I told you so!*

"Your interview," Mr. Witt says. "You drove all the way to Bowling Green just to audition."

"You might have a *job* for me?"

Kaylee rolls her eyes.

Mr. Witt says, "That depends on how far you're willing to go."

"I'll do anything."

"I wonder if that's true."

"Put me to the test."

"Are you busy right now?"

"Not if you've got a challenge for me."

"How fast can you get to Candlewood Plaza?"

"Twenty minutes, give or take."

"Meet me in the courtyard."

"How should I dress?"

"Suit jacket and pants, no tie."

"Thank you so much, Mr. Witt! You won't be sorry!"

"Whatever."

Bobby hangs up, looks at Kaylee and says, "You were right."

"I *told* you!"

"He wants to meet me at Candlewood Plaza in 20 minutes. Said he couldn't give me details on the phone."

"I can tell you what he wants."

"How much can you tell in five minutes?"

"Everything I know."

"Let's hear it."

"There are lots of people involved in this TV thing. Some are called talent, some are labor. Apparently, you're labor. There's also a beautiful young actress with no experience who agreed to have sex with a guy from labor in return for a starring role."

"So how does that affect me?"

"You're the guy."

"The one who gets to have sex with the actress?"

She frowns. "Try not to act too excited, will you?"

"Sorry. It's just a bit of a shock. Why me?"

"There's a catch."

Bobby groans. "Of course there is." He sighs deeply. "What's the fine print?"

"Actually, it's all great for you. You're gonna have sex with two women on two successive nights: the beautiful actress, and another challenger."

"Who's the challenger?"

"Ivy."

"*What?*"

She nods.

"I don't understand. What am I missing?"

"Ivy and the actress are competing for your vote. Whichever one you rate higher gets a huge bonus."

"Why would I have sex with Ivy? I'm furious with her!"

"That's the whole point. Ivy's gonna have to work her ass off to get a higher rating. She'll have to win you over despite the fact you're mad at her."

"Not going to happen. I'm not going to do it."

"I think you will."

"Give me one good reason."

"I'll give you two. First is bragging rights. The producers think the show's gonna be huge."

"So?"

"Imagine being able to say you slept with Nicole Kidman or Gwyneth Paltrow before they became mega stars."

Bobby shrugs. "What's the second reason?"

"They're gonna pay you ten grand."

Bobby's jaw drops. "No shit?"

"That's what he said."

He shows her a sly smile. "If I do it, are you going to be jealous?"

"Of course." She pauses a beat, then says, "But I'll get over it."

Bobby chuckles. "Maybe we *could* have a future together!"

"I'm not happy about this situation, but the plain fact is we haven't started dating yet, and you need the money. But after tomorrow, if we *do* start dating, I'll expect you to be faithful."

He grins. "Damn! Just when I thought I'd found the perfect girl!"

She punches his arm playfully. "I'll keep you happy. You'll see."

She stands.

"Wait," he says. "I'll walk you to your car."

On the porch, he says, "It won't be much of a contest."

"Why's that?"

"Ivy's got no chance. I'm pissed at her. I already want the starlet to win."

"You won't be able to tell them apart."

"What are you *talking* about? I've already *know* Ivy. I've *been* with her."

"Try not to remind me. But anyway, you'll be wearing a hood over your head."

"*That's* weird. But I'll still be able to tell them apart. I'm sure Ivy's hips are wider than the starlet's."

"I'm sure you're right. But your hands are gonna be cuffed to your headboard same as last night. You're going to basically lie on your back. The girls are gonna do all the work."

Bobby looks skeptical.

"What now?"

"I know Ivy's scent."

Kaylee wrinkles her nose. "Eew! Try not to be gross, okay?"

"Huh? Wait...Oh! No, I'm talking about her perfume. Her breath. Her hair, her—"

"Let it go, Bobby."

"Okay. Sorry."

"Look. Ivy and the starlet are gonna be wearing the same perfume. They'll use the same shampoo. Same toothpaste, same mouthwash, same deodorant. Mr. Witt will probably come up with a dozen things to throw you off your game. You really won't be able to tell which is which. That's the whole point. And you can bet the producers are hoping you'll choose Ivy."

"Why?"

"According to Mr. Witt, it's better TV."

She watches his face as he plays it out in his mind. Then she says, "Do you have any idea how many guys would kill to be in your position? Two women trying as hard as they can to get your vote?"

"A hundred million?"

"At least. And they'd do it for free."

"Not me."

She smiles, kisses his cheek. "I better go. Act surprised when he tells you."

As they walk to Kaylee's car, Bobby says, "Which girl's coming tonight?"

"Which one's cumming? That's an interesting way to put it. I have no idea, nor do they. After they cuff you, Mr. Witt's gonna flip a coin."

"Why?"

"He wants to give Ivy a fair shot at the money.

"But *you'll* know."

"What do you mean?"

"Later on tonight. You'll know if I was with Ivy or the starlet."

"I'm sure I will. So?"

"Will you call and tell me?"

"Let's exchange phone numbers now, while we're thinking about it."

"Good idea."

They do, then Bobby says, "So you'll call me afterward? To tell me who I wound up banging tonight?"

"No."

"Why not? Don't you want to punish Ivy?"

"She'll be punished enough when she learns how happy we are as a couple."

He looks away for a moment. "I don't suppose..." He glances sideways at her, then shakes his head and says, "Never mind."

"What?"

"It's not important."

She frowns. "I hate it when people do that. I wish you'd just come out and say whatever's on your mind. It's so much better to be straightforward."

Bobby sighs. "Okay. It's just...for a split second it crossed my mind to wonder if Mr. Witt paid you to come here and tell me all this."

"*Excuse* me?"

"If he did, it's fine. I'd just like to know."

She grits her teeth. "He didn't. And nor would it make sense. I'm disappointed you'd even think that."

"I'm sorry. It's just that so many crazy things have happened in the past 24 hours, it's hard to know who or what to believe."

"I'll make it easy for you. You can believe anything I tell you. As for being confused, I think that's the whole point of the reality show. You're *supposed* to be confused. You're looking at me funny again."

"I..."

"Let me guess. You don't know me very well, and I could be lying. Someone could have paid me to swear I'm telling the truth, right?"

He shrugs.

"I get that, Bobby, and it doesn't really matter if you believe me or not. I just wanted you to know what was happening, because if I were in your situation I'd want to know. And I hope by telling you this it's not gonna come back and bite me on the ass."

"It won't."

"Just for the record, I swear I've never spoken to Mr. Witt other than to let him in the apartment this morning. I also swear on my life that Ivy has no idea I'm telling you any of this."

"I believe you. I'm sorry I said it. I won't tell anyone you spoke to me."

She gets in the car, but leaves the door open, as if something's been left unsaid.

"What's wrong?"

Kaylee glances at the front door, bites her lip, then fixes her gaze on Bobby. "How long has your housekeeper been working for you?"

"Just a few weeks."

"How well do you know her?"

"Not that well. Why?"

"You think she could be involved?"

"*Kennon?* How?"

"Her being a housekeeper doesn't fit. But you know what does?"

He shakes his head.

"It fits that she might be the beautiful actress who's willing to sleep with you to land the starring role."

Bobby allows himself a split second to consider her theory. Could it possibly be true?

Sadly, no, and he tells her why: "My parents hired Kennon, remember? And they know nothing about the reality show."

"Have you asked your parents how they found her?"

"Not really."

"Don't you think you should?"

She puts her hand out, as if to shake. He brushes it aside, leans into the car, gives her a hug. I agree with you."

"About what?"

"We have high potential as a couple."

She smiles. "Assuming you don't fall in love with Ivy after she gives you another ride."

"Fat chance."

Kaylee arches an eyebrow. "She prefers the word curvy."

"Ouch," he says.

He smiles, gives her a quick kiss on the lips.

She extends the kiss, takes his hand, places it on her boob, and says, "To be continued."

She blushes at her boldness, starts the car, and backs out of the driveway, completely oblivious to the blonde in the black sedan parked 50 yards away who's been watching Bobby's house for the past hour. The one who's come to the conclusion a careful inspection of the inside of Bobby's house is warranted.

Chapter 13

BOBBY WAITS TILL Kaylee's out of sight before making the call.

"Hello?"

"Hi Dad."

"Hi son. Uh, I should tell you straight away if you need some cash, I'm afraid I can't help you till next month."

"I'm good, Dad."

"You sure?"

"Positive."

"Okay. Still, if you need some help next month, don't hesitate to call."

"Thanks. You're amazing. I'm actually calling about the housekeeper."

"Is there a problem? Has something happened?"

"No. She's terrific."

"Glad to hear it. You had me worried a minute. What about her?"

"Uh...have you ever met her?"

"No."

"Ever seen a photograph?"

"Why? Is there something wrong with her?"

"Quite the opposite."

"She's a looker?" He chuckles. "Well, that's a plus, isn't it?"

"Can I ask how much you're paying her?"

"You can, but I won't answer."

"Why not?"

"She's a gift from your mom and me."

"But—"

"Stop a minute. You remember that autographed baseball you gave me last year? I know you spent a small fortune on it, but I'd never insult you by asking for details."

"I understand that. It's just that I know you're on a fixed income, and this housekeeper has got to be costing you a ton. To tell you the truth, I'm thinking about letting her go."

"Please don't do that. It's really not a burden, financially."

"That can't be true. And anyway, whatever you're spending, I'd rather you use it to take care of yourselves."

Bobby's dad pauses a long time before saying, "Look, I'm not supposed to tell you this, but Megan arranged for your mom and me to get a substantial check each month."

"*What?* My *wife* is sending you money?"

"Relax. She apparently came into a large sum of money recently and wanted to do something nice for us. She established an annuity in our names. I told her we couldn't accept it, but she said it was a done deal, and the money was coming whether we used it or not. She said if we refused to use it for ourselves, maybe we could use it to help you. So your mother came up with the idea of hiring a full-service housekeeper. One who cooks and does the grocery shopping and keeps the house tidy."

"You're in Arizona."

"So?"

"Who gave you the lead for the housekeeper?"

"Uh...we didn't actually make the arrangements."

"Who did?"

"Megan's secretary. When I called Megan to tell her how we planned to use the money she thought it was a great idea. She said she'd have her secretary make some calls. Uh...she's not stealing from you, is she?"

"No Dad."

"Good. Then there's nothing left to discuss. We've spoken to her, you know. Your mom and me."

"You spoke to Kennon?"

"We did. And just so you know, she's very happy working for you. Says you're neat and extremely thoughtful."

"Did she ever mention a man named Mr. Witt?"

"Not to me."

"Thanks, Dad."

"It's our pleasure, Son."

Bobby looks up to see Kennon standing on the porch looking every bit the gorgeous movie star he hopes she is.

"Is everything okay?" she asks in a voice that seems far sexier than he remembered.

He says nothing. Just looks at her while silently praying she's the one who's going to be all over him tonight.

Chapter 14

Andrew Witt and Bobby Tang.

BOBBY FINDS MR. Witt sitting on a bench in the Candlewood Plaza courtyard.

"Were you able to get the company to cut my check?" Bobby says.

Mr. Witt hands him a piece of paper.

"What's this?"

"Your FedEx tracking number. You'll have it by 10:00 a.m. tomorrow."

Bobby studies the paper a moment, then says, "Thanks for doing that."

"My pleasure." He motions Bobby to sit beside him.

As he does, Bobby says, "What was it you said earlier? I've lost my *mojo*?"

"I believe you have. At your initial interview in Bowling Green you told us Megan used to idolize you."

"She did. In the early days."

"Back then you were her Superman?"

"I guess."

"But she turned out to be your kryptonite. Your marriage counselor told you to make her feel appreciated."

"She said to help out with the housework, and be more romantic. So I put love notes in her underwear drawer, chocolates and rose petals on her pillow, and—"

"You turned into a pussy."

Bobby frowns. "I wouldn't put it *that* way."

"Well, you *should*, because it was the exact wrong advice."

"I agree. You know what Megan said? She said, 'If you think it impresses me to see you doing dishes and washing clothes you're dead wrong. If you think it excites me to see my lover turn into my house boy you obviously know nothing about women.'"

"She stopped respecting you."

Bobby nods, and silently asks himself how it's possible that the mere mention of Megan's name is enough to override his excitement over the possibility of having sex with Kennon and a relationship with Kaylee.

Mr. Witt says, "You know why Megan stopped respecting you?"

"Because I lost my mojo?"

"That's right. To her you went from Superman to Clark Kent." He stares into Bobby's eyes. "Are you happy being Clark Kent?"

"Fuck no!"

"You know what I think? I think it's time you regained your position on the food chain. I think it's time to reassert yourself and become the alpha male Megan fell in love with years ago."

"I assume you've got something in mind. I'm willing to hear it."

Mr. Witt shakes his head. "I'm afraid it'll take more guts than you've got."

"I'll do whatever it takes."

"You'd have to reinvent yourself."

"What do you mean?"

"You need to get meat in your diet. Need to get in the hunt and stir the primal juices. Need to get your adrenalin going."

"I'm hearing a lot of words, but no plan."

"You *cannot* regain Megan's affection by adapting to *her* environment. You need to create your *own* environment and let *her* do the adapting."

"How?"

"By separating yourself from the herd."

"Right. But *how*?"

"By doing something *spectacular*! Something that represents ultimate control. Ultimate power."

Bobby shakes his head in frustration. "I have no idea what you're talking about."

Mr. Witt turns his head right, then left, then lowers his voice to a whisper and says, "I'm talking about taking a human life."

Chapter 15

"*WHAT?*" BOBBY SAYS. "You want me to *kill* someone?"

"Megan can never know, of course, nor will she need to because the change in your attitude will become instantly apparent to her. The thrill of the kill puts you right back in the jungle."

"You're mad!"

"Once you kill a man for the sheer sport of it, you'll become a person of unlimited power. Committing a murder, a *perfect* murder, can change the course of your life."

"How?"

"It'll force you to regain the fire she saw in you. Women can sense a man with confidence. They *love*...a man with confidence. And a man who's killed a man? Well, you can't help but exude confidence. Within seconds you'll go from marshmallow to man of action; a man of mystery, with attitude. A man with a secret. A man who exudes that singular confidence that comes from knowing you have the ability to take another man's life. It's an intoxicating feeling of power, and one that can overcome any obstacle the Megans of the world try to dump in your path."

Bobby stares at Mr. Witt a long time before saying, "This is a joke, right?"

"No, Bobby, it's the real deal, and the best chance you have of winning Megan. With all that adrenalin, testosterone, and alpha power coursing through your body, she'll view you like an addict views crack. You'll stop whining; stop begging her to come back to you. You'll win her back, and do you know why?"

Bobby shakes his head.

"Because there's a primal gene in every woman's brain, a need to feel secure and protected. And there's a primal gene in every man's brain, a kill-or-be-killed directive that is absolutely intoxicating to women. Did you *hear* me Bobby? I said you'll *win* her back, not *beg* her to come back."

"What you're saying—"

"What I'm saying is there are millions of miserable sons of bitches in the world who are going to die one way or the other. Thousands will die in the next 15 minutes whether you kill one or not. But if you want the kind of confidence that knows no bounds, the kind of confidence that turns you into an irresistible man of power, the kind of confidence that lifts you up and will not let you down—one of these miserable assholes has to die."

Bobby says, "No. What you're really saying is in *your* depraved mind, killing a total stranger is a fair trade for improving your outlook. This is a human *being* we're talking about. He could have a *family*."

Mr. Witt does a double-take, as if he can't believe his ears. "You think the lion pauses to think about the gazelle's family? You think he agonizes over the repercussions of the attack? Of course not. He lives in the moment. He strikes suddenly, viciously, powerfully. He's the one others want to be, and the one the females want to be with. Think about what it means to be a lion, Bobby. To be the predator, not the prey."

"I *am* thinking about it, and what I'm thinking is—even if I find a way to slough off all the moral issues—I'd get caught. You see, I'm *already* one of those miserable sons of bitches you're talking about. But you know what would make me even *more* miserable? Serving a life sentence for murder."

Mr. Witt smiles. "Ask yourself one simple question."

"What's that?"

"What would you attempt to do if it were impossible to fail?"

Bobby coughs out a laugh. "I certainly wouldn't attempt murder!"

"No? What if it were impossible to get caught? What if I could guarantee it?"

"Sorry pal. I've seen too many TV shows. I'd absolutely get caught. First of all, I don't know a damned thing about killing people. Second, I wouldn't have the guts. Third—"

"Back up, Bobby. You won't get caught. I guarantee it. And you don't need to know anything about killing people because the way you'll do it is as easy as passing the salt. As for not having the guts, I agree: you don't. But the moment you complete the challenge you'll have the courage to do anything your heart desires. Because once you've taken a human life, no person or situation can intimidate you. Your brain will retain the stored knowledge of what you've accomplished, and everything else will seem trivial. It's a powerful feeling, Bobby. One you can't fathom; a high from which you'll never come down."

"I suppose the next thing you'll tell me is *you've* killed a man."

"I've killed a number of people, Bobby. Men and women alike."

Bobby smirks. "I find that awfully hard to believe."

"Do you? Tell me this: which of us is younger?"

"I am."

"Stronger?"

"Me."

"Better looking?"

"Definitely me."

"More confident?"

Bobby pauses. "You."

"By a wide margin, wouldn't you say?"

Bobby shrugs.

Mr. Witt says, "Funny, don't you think?"

"What's that?"

"You appear to have everything going for you, and I appear to have nothing going for me, but I have 100 times more confidence than you. Know why?"

"You've killed people?"

"That's right. And when I show you how easy it is you won't doubt me in the least. When I tell you the plan you'll know what I know."

"Which is what, exactly?"

"Killing a man can be quicker and easier than taking a shit."

Bobby looks around. "I don't see the cameras."

"There aren't any."

"I know how you work. Everything's smoke and mirrors. This whole thing is bullshit. You're testing me, trying to see how I'll react. But here's your answer: there's no way you're going to convince me that killing a man will help my relationship with Megan."

"Does that mean you don't even want me to tell you how to commit the perfect murder?"

Bobby gives him a look. "I didn't say *that*."

"Let's put it all on the line, shall we? What's the one thing you desire most in the world?"

"Megan."

"What if I can arrange that?"

"You don't even *know* her."

"I know how to get you and Megan face to face. Maybe from there you can make your pitch."

"She won't even take my calls!"

"Doesn't matter. She'll take mine."

"Why?"

"How about *I* concentrate on that and *you* concentrate on being the kind of man Megan wants."

"I'd rather hear your plan for contacting Megan, and getting her to meet me."

"I have connections, Bobby. I can present you in a whole different light."

"Give me a for instance."

"What if I could get you an acting role?"

"In a porn reality show?" He laughs. "Megan would never speak to me again if she knew what I did last night for cash."

"She won't have to know about that, or what you're going to be doing the next couple of days. But I'm talking about a real movie."

"Hollywood?"

"It could be arranged."

"If I'm willing to kill someone."

"That's right."

"For the sake of argument...Who would I have to kill?"

"The first person you see."

"*What?*"

"Well, obviously, it would have to be someone you don't know. It'll have to be a perfect stranger, and it'll have to be quick."

"Okay, I'll play along. You see that guy by the flagpole talking to the old lady? What am I supposed to do, pull out a gun and shoot them?"

"No. Not out in the open. You need an enclosed space with no witnesses."

"Such as?"

"A men's room."

"I'm supposed to shoot a guy while he's taking a piss?"

"You won't be shooting anyone. It's too noisy."

"What about a silencer?"

"Forget what you've seen on TV. A gun and silencer are too large to conceal. And if you carry them separately you'd need time to assemble them."

"A knife?"

"No, Bobby. Anything that causes blood to spurt is a bad idea. Blood evidence will land you in prison faster than Manti Te'o falls in love."

"What, I'm supposed to club him to death?"

"You really *are* bad at this. Once again, you've described an attack that generates copious quantities of blood. Not only that, but lots of victims survive beatings so severe they can't offer up a pulse. You know what they call those types of victims?"

"What?"

"Witnesses."

Bobby spreads his hands, palms up. "Fine. I give up. How would *you* kill a guy in a men's room?"

Mr. Witt produces a tiny spray bottle. "Ever seen one of these?"

"Yeah. My dad carries one. It's some sort of nitro spray in case he gets chest pains."

"That's right. Except that in this case, it's the murder weapon."

"What's in it?"

"A mixture of cyanide and DMSO."

"What's that?"

"Dimethyl sulfoxide. You spray this into a guy's face, he's dead in 38 seconds."

"That's impossible."

"I've used it many times, and others have, too. But I'll go you one step further. Spray this in a stranger's face in the next 15 minutes and I'll not only get you a movie role, I'll also let you fuck a movie star tonight. Six points total. Plus,

I'll find a way to reunite you and Megan. You have my word."

"Sixty grand?"

"That's right. Fifty for spraying the guy, ten for fucking the starlet. Details to follow."

"What if the spray doesn't work?"

"I'm confident it will."

"Of course you are. But what if it doesn't? What if something goes wrong?"

"I'll be right outside the men's room, guarding the door. If you have the slightest problem, I'll take over."

"If it's that easy, why don't *you* do it?"

"I'll do it if I have to, or finish the job if you screw up. But the show isn't based on what *I* can do. It's based on what I can get others to do."

"You're planning to kill a person on TV?"

"No, but we have to be able to sell it. If I can get you to do it in real life we'll know it's plausible. When we film the show we'll use a different scenario, but the motivation will be the same."

"Or you'll find someone else?"

"That's right. It shouldn't be hard to find a guy who'll take sixty grand for fucking a movie star and squirting some liquid into a stranger's face. You agree?"

Bobby looks around the courtyard a minute, then says, "Where's the bathroom?"

Mr. Witt points to one of the buildings. "We'll enter the lobby, make sure the bathroom's empty, then wait a short distance away. When the first guy goes in we'll walk to the door. You'll go in, I'll stand guard."

"First guy who's not wearing a wedding ring."

Mr. Witt sighs. "If you insist."

"How would I squirt the guy?"

"He should be standing at the urinal. If he's not, you'll come back out and we'll try again. If he *is* at the urinal you'll pretend you're going to use the one beside him. As you step up to it you'll ask, "Do I know you?" He'll turn, and you'll squirt him in the face."

"How many times?"

"Once or twice. No more. And make sure before entering you've got the nozzle aimed away from you."

"That's it?"

"Yeah. Except that when you squirt him, hold your breath, then back away quickly, so you won't inhale the fumes."

"Will I be in any danger?"

"Only if you inhale the fumes."

"What if he screams?"

"He won't be able to. All you have to do is squirt him. When he falls to the floor, leave."

"And you'll be guarding the door?"

"I'll do more than that. I'll stay at the door and block it until you get out of sight."

"What do I do with the bottle?"

"Give it to me when you exit the bathroom."

Bobby thinks about it. Then says, "I'd like to hear details about the movie star."

"Two women have agreed to have sex with you. One's a movie star, the other's your old friend, Ivy."

"*Ivy?* How'd you find *her?*" Bobby says, attempting to put the right amount of surprise in his voice.

"She was easy enough to track down. At any rate, you'll have sex with one of them tonight, and the other one tomorrow. Then you're going to rate them. Whoever you rate higher gets a bonus of fifty grand. You can see where this is going, right? You're probably angry at Ivy, so she's going to have to work really hard to get your vote. You should pay *us* for this challenge."

"I assume the movie star's clean?"

"Of course. We'd never put your health at risk."

"You put my health at risk with Ivy."

"*You* put your health at risk with Ivy. Your challenge was to seduce any young lady who happened along. Was Ivy the first girl who stopped to check on you?"

"No."

"That's right. *You* chose *her.*"

"I did. What if I say no?"

"There's no need to feel obligated. The only reason we're talking is because you asked for additional work. I told you I'd see what I could do, and this is it. But you're not the only guy we signed for this project. We held interviews in twelve cities. If you're not interested I'll give these challenges to the next guy. Trust me; they can all use an extra sixty grand."

"You said this has to happen in the next 15 minutes?"

"That's right."

"Why? Are you afraid if I think about it I'll back out?"

"Doesn't matter what I think. Ball's in your court, Bobby. What's it going to be?"

Bobby bites his lip. "Can I check out the layout of the bathroom before making my decision?"

"Let's go."

Chapter 16

Kennon Tate.

BOBBY LEFT THE house ten minutes ago. It's early afternoon, and Kennon's been working nonstop since freeing him from his handcuffs. With the house in good shape, and no appetite for the sandwich she brought, she stands by the sink and looks out the window while enjoying a cup of coffee. When she's finished, she rinses it out. A sudden flash of movement catches her eye, and she looks out the window in time to see two squirrels fucking in the front yard. She frowns, remembering how our government wasted $600,000 of taxpayer money this year to research the sex habits of South African ground squirrels.

Although she's only worked for him a couple of weeks, Kennon knows every sound the house makes when she's here alone. Not only that, but she keeps the doors locked at all times, even when Bobby's in the house. In addition, her hearing and intuition is second to none. For these reasons and others, if you were to ask her at this very moment, she'd say there's no way a gorgeous young blonde with piercing gray eyes could possibly be standing behind her, pointing a gun at the back of her head.

Which is why Kennon screams bloody murder when the voice behind her says, "Don't scream."

The blonde's eyes show she's not happy about the screaming.

Kennon forces herself quiet. "What do you want?"

Without moving the gun, the blonde nods at the kitchen table. "Sit."

Kennon takes a seat.

The blonde lowers the gun to her side, but stands over her. "Who are you?"

"Kennon Tate."

"And what's your relationship to Bobby Tang?"

"I'm his housekeeper."

"His housekeeper."

Kennon nods.

The blonde says, "Look at me. Study my face." She pauses a moment, then says, "Do I look like Black Kettle?"

"Who?"

"Chief of the Cheyenne? Eighteen-sixties? Chief of the Council of Forty-Four?"

"I'm sorry. I have no idea what you're talking about."

"How about Joe Paterno?"

"Excuse me?"

"You know who he was?"

"Yes."

"Study me carefully. My face, my body. Is there any way I could pass for Joe Paterno?"

Bewildered by the conversation, Kennon shakes her head no.

The blonde nods. "How about Billy Graham?"

"I'm sorry. No."

"Emmett Love? Nelson Mandela?"

Kennon shakes her head.

The blonde says, "You're right, by the way. I couldn't pass for any of these people. Now tell me why."

"Uh...Because you're not a man?"

"You're missing the point. Could anyone mistake me for Mother Teresa?"

"No."

"Why?"

"Because you're young?"

"What else?"

"You're beautiful? You're alive? You're American?"

The blonde sighs. "Let me help you with this. I can't pass for anyone who exemplifies high integrity. It's just not who I am. You can tell that by looking at me, can't you?"

"I-I'd rather not say."

The blonde smiles, but there's no warmth in it. "My point is I'm not a person of integrity, and you're not a housekeeper. Now check your watch."

Kennon's eyes go to her wrist watch, then to the blonde's face.

The blonde says, "From this moment in time, you and I are going to be completely honest with each other. I'll prove my sincerity by going first: I'm Callie Carpenter, and I'm a contract killer."

Kennon's eyes go wide.

Callie says, "People are going to die in this house to-night, Kennon, but you don't have to be one of them. Not if you're completely honest with me." She pauses a moment, then says, "What time are you done here today?"

"Five."

Callie says, "We'll need to talk about that. But before we do, I want you to know that physical beauty is something I revere, especially in the female form. You're astonishingly pretty, Kennon, and if circumstances were different, I'd do everything possible to protect you. But due to the nature of my business today, that won't be my first concern. But I will make you a promise: if you lie to me now, and I have to take your life tonight, I won't mar your features with a knife, acid, flames, or bullet holes. You understand?"

Kennon nods.

Callie says, "Your corpse will be intact; your face, beau-tiful. Say thank you."

"Thank you."

"Now it's your turn to talk."

"What would you like to know?"

"Everything. But let's start with this: who the fuck *are* you, and why are you here?"

Chapter 17

NAT BAILEY KEEPS bath oil beads in a miniature bottle in the desk drawer of his office. Around this time every afternoon, Nat opens the bottle, removes a bath bead, pops it in his mouth, swallows it.

Nat isn't eating soap.

The bath beads have been carefully hollowed out, cleaned, and refilled with crystal meth, surrounded by ecstasy. Known on the street as a *Madonna and Child*, the X is released first, then the meth. If Nat runs out of bath beads he can always *parachute* the drugs, meaning he can wrap them in a pinch of toilet paper before swallowing, to cut the horrendously bitter taste.

Nat loves his meth. Loves how it makes him feel euphoric, invincible, confident. Loves the speed and endurance it brings. When tweaking, Nat transforms into his alter ego, *Nat Supersonic*, a superhuman who functions at warp speed.

He leans back in his chair, closes his eyes, waits for the drug to work its magic. Users claim it takes 30 minutes for oral-dosed meth to kick in, and 40 for X, but everyone's different. In Nat's experience X takes 20 minutes, max. He uses it to suppress his emotional insecurities. Put better, when rolling on X, Nat has zero fear of female rejection.

Ellen, his secretary, interrupts him with a muffled knocking sound at his door. He ignores it, but she enters his office anyway, carrying a thick file. "May I speak to you a moment?"

He shrugs.

She closes the door, sits in one of the two chairs in front of his desk, stares at his face a moment, frowns, and says, "Can we play *You Should?*"

"Make it quick."

She places the file on his desk, takes a deep breath. "*You should*...get started on the Gilchrest file."

"Because?"

"It's a test. It's make-or-break for you."

"My job's on the line?"

"That's my understanding."

"Says who?"

"Juno's secretary."

He nods. "Thanks for the heads up. What about you?"

"Apparently my job is safe either way."

"Noted. My turn. "*You should*...lose 20 pounds."

Ellen frowns. "Because?"

"You'd go from interesting to hot."

"Noted. Number two: *You should*...be more careful what you say to Carl Roemer over drinks."

"Because?"

"He's a scandalmonger."

Nat laughs. "Great word! *Scandalmonger.* I like that. What's he saying?"

"That you're having an affair."

"Fuck. Who's he told?"

"Everyone who'll listen."

Nat frowns. "Noted. Number two: *You should...*put yourself up for a raise before I get canned."

"Because?"

"I'll approve any reasonable request. You've been loyal when you didn't need to be, and I appreciate it."

"Noted. Thank you."

His cell phone vibrates. He glances at it, then checks his watch.

She looks at him. "Are you okay?"

"Sure. Fine. Are we done?"

"One more. *You should....*"

"Yes?"

"Get off the drugs. People are starting to take notice. If Juno finds out—"

He waves her off. "Noted. Number three: *You should...*mind your own business. We're done here. Please close the door behind you on your way out."

Ellen sighs. "Noted." She gets to her feet slowly; gives him a sad look, leaves the room.

Nat closes his eyes, waits for the drug's embrace. When it comes, he jumps to his feet, darts his eyes around the room like a squirrel in a dog park. When his focus settles on the Gilchrest file he opens it, fans the papers across the entire length of his desktop, pulls his dick out and and soaks them with piss.

Laughing maniacally, he bounds across the room, throws the door open, shouts, "I'll be back when I'm back!"

"Tuck in," Ellen says, frowning, pointing at his fly.

"Noted!"

Nat's in complete control. He's a social user, not an addict, and proves the difference twice a day by ingesting his drugs orally. Unlike addicts who snort, smoke, or inject their meth, Nat has the discipline to wait for his high. Oral is slower, but safer. No rotted teeth, emaciated face, brain damage, or death in *his* future!

He spies an open elevator and runs to it with the wild abandon of a kid on a scavenger hunt. Presses the button and waits an eternity for it to arrive at the first floor lobby. When it does, he rushes to the front of the building and searches the courtyard.

No dealer.

He checks his phone:

H. Bathroom. Dorfman-Beck building.

He race-walks across the courtyard, keeping his speed just short of a trot, so no one will think he's acting weird.

His phone vibrates again. He checks the text: *Where are you?*

On my way! he texts.

Two weeks ago Nat waited for more than an hour in the pouring rain for his old dealer, but Seppi never showed. Turns out he got busted. But in a stroke of amazing good fortune, the police never confiscated Seppi's contacts, and they've been passed on to the next guy in the chain. A guy who calls himself Mr. W, who's bringing the heroin Nat requested.

He climbs the steps to the Dorfman-Beck lobby, walks the hall till he locates the men's room. Finds it empty and realizes—what else is new?—he needs to take a quick piss. It's probably a false alarm, since he emptied his bladder on his desk moments ago. Still, he's here, so why not give it a go?

He steps up to one of the urinals and assumes the pose. Seconds later, a guy comes in, takes the urinal beside him, and says, "Do I know you?"

Nat turns, sees a tiny spray bottle aimed at his eyes. Before he can duck away, a spritz of fine mist covers his face. Nat instinctively starts to back away, but his legs give out. He slips and crashes to the floor. Lies there with his eyes bugging out, hissing like a garter snake.

Chapter 18

BOBBY'S SO GRATEFUL to see Mr. Witt standing guard outside the bathroom door he gives him a bear hug.

"Thanks," Mr. Witt says. "But you need to get moving."

"Right."

Bobby releases him, hands over the canister. Mr. Witt says, "Good job. I heard him hit the floor. Go home, I'll meet you in half an hour."

"You think he's dead?"

"I know he is. Otherwise, he'd be screaming. Look, you're numb, in a bit of shock, so be sure to drive safely, okay?"

"Am I going to prison?"

"No Bobby, you're going home. Make sure your house-keeper sees you."

"Why?"

"It'll establish your whereabouts, in case anyone happens to see you here. And Bobby?"

"Yeah?"

"You really should get moving. You just killed a man, and we're in an office building. Someone will need to piss before long."

Bobby nods, absently. "I'm going home now?"

"You are. I'll meet you in half an hour."

Bobby walks away in a daze, much slower than Mr. Witt anticipated. Nevertheless, he remains by the door, as promised, till Bobby's out of sight. Then he enters the bathroom, checks out the guy on the floor. He nudges the body with his toe and stares at him for a full 15 seconds before saying, "You can get up now, Nat."

Nat opens his eyes and does a double-take, "*Andrew?* What the *fuck?*"

Mr. Witt smiles. "Say hello to your new drug dealer."

"My...*what?* That can't be *true!* We're *neighbors!*"

Mr. Witt shrugs, opens the cabinet door below the sink, removes the folded *Out of Order* sign. He opens the bathroom door, sets the sign up in front of it, then re-enters the bathroom and wedges a portable lock into the strike plate before closing it, effectively locking them inside.

Nat, still on the floor, but sitting, says, "How can you possibly deal *drugs?* I've known you for two years!"

"Want to keep your voice down a bit?"

"Right. Yes, of course. Sorry. Jesus, Andrew." He gets to his feet, takes a deep breath, stares into the eyes of the last person on earth he'd believe to be a drug dealer. "How long have you known?"

"About your habit? Since the day we met. Don't look so surprised. It's my business."

"Your voice sounded familiar just now, but when I looked up and saw it was you, I nearly shit! I literally had no idea."

"Good. I must be doing my job well."

"You're the number two guy?"

"Actually, Seppi was *my* number two guy."

"No *shit?*" Nat shakes his head. "I had no idea."

"You said that already."

"Does Betty know you're a dealer?"

Mr. Witt frowns. "You're impossible to deal with when you're high. I'll ask you one last time to keep your voice down."

"Sorry."

"No."

"Excuse me?"

"Betty doesn't know."

Nat nods. Says, "I usually see her at the gym, or walking around the neighborhood. But not lately."

"She's at her mother's, in Johnson City."

"Everything all right?"

"Her mom had a stroke. Betty's helping out."

"Please give her my best."

"I'll do that."

Nat dusts himself off. "Did your client buy it?"

"I think so."

"Good. Can I ask why you wanted him to think he killed me?"

"Not important. How about we fast-forward the conversation to why we're here."

Nat's eyes light up. "You brought the H?"

Mr. Witt smiles.

Nat's eyes follow his hand as he reaches into his pocket. Except that what he removes isn't heroin, it's another canister. Before Nat can react, Mr. Witt sprays his face. Nat shudders violently, and slumps onto the sink as if all the bones have been removed from his body. Then, like a giant ship sinking into the ocean's depths, Nat slips ever-so-slowly to the floor. Now, lying on his back, his mouth quakes open and shut like a fresh-caught bass trying to fill its lungs with air. His mouth does that a while, then stops. His eyes are open, bugging out, same as they were when Bobby sprayed him.

Only this time he's dead.

Before leaving the crime scene, Mr. Witt confiscates Nat's phone, then stretches his body out, pulls his pants and underwear to his ankles. Takes two photos: one, the entire body; and two, a close-up of Nat's penis. He leaves him like that, then removes the portable lock and exits the room. Places the Out of Order sign directly in front of the door. Then walks down the hall toward the lobby while entering a code on his cell phone. When the answering machine beeps he says, "Betty? I have to run a quick errand. I know you're starving, but soon as I'm done, I'll bring you something to eat. Sorry for the delay. Love you!"

Mr. Witt exits the Dorfman-Beck building, makes his way through the parking lot to his car, climbs in, fires up the engine. When he gets to Bobby's house the front door is slightly open. He enters to find four people standing in the living room: Bobby, Kennon the housekeeper, and two police detectives.

Chapter 19

"WHO'RE YOU?" one of the detectives asks.

"Friend of the family," Mr. Witt says.

"This doesn't concern you."

"I'm also Bobby's attorney."

The detectives look at each other, exchange a look of disgust. Detective Brewer turns to Bobby. "Is that right?"

Bobby says, "Mr. Witt, these are detectives Brewer and King. Detectives, this is my...*attorney*, Andrew Witt."

Mr. Witt nods. "Please continue your questioning. Pretend I'm not here. I'll let you know if you overstep your bounds."

Detective Brewer's unhappy, but it could be worse. Most attorneys wouldn't allow a discussion to take place at all. He says, "I was asking your client about his wife."

"Can I see your badges?"

"Huh?"

"Your badges. I assume you've shown them to Bobby, but I'd feel better seeing them myself."

While they fumble for badges, Mr. Witt says, "Nice to see *you* again, Kennon."

She nods without changing expression, while instinctively crossing her arms over her breasts.

When Detectives Brewer and King show their badges Mr. Witt says, "Thank you. Please continue."

Brewer says, "When's the last time you saw Megan?"

"I already told you. About eight weeks ago, or something like that. Why do you keep asking?"

"Because it's my job. How long have you two been legally separated?"

"Since the last time I saw her."

"Eight weeks?"

Bobby nods.

"And during those eight weeks how many times has she entered your home?"

"None. It's one of the conditions of the separation."

Brewer turns his attention to Kennon. "You've worked here how long?"

"A little over two weeks."

"Every day?"

"Three times a week."

"Ever met Mrs. Tang?"

"No sir."

"Ever seen her in the house?"

"No sir."

"And she's not here now?"

"*Here?*"

"The attic? The basement?"

Kennon's eyes go big. "You think she might be living here without our knowledge?"

"*Our* knowledge?"

"Me and Mr. Tang."

"*You* don't live here, do you?"

"No sir."

"Ever spend the night?"

She looks at Bobby. "Of course not!"

King says, "That'll be all, Miss Tate. We'll holler if we need to ask you anything else."

All four men watch Kennon leave the room. "Lucky you," Brewer says.

"Has something happened to Megan?"

"We're not sure. Right now we're pursuing leads."

"For what?"

"She's been reported missing."

"By whom?"

Detective Brewer looks at his partner. "That's an odd question to ask, don't you think?"

King says, "My first question would be, 'Are you sure?' or I might say, 'Oh, my God!' But he's only interested in *who* reported her. Yeah, I'd say that's odd. And suspicious."

Bobby clarifies, "What I mean is we're separated. I'd have no way of knowing if she was missing or not. She travels a 500-mile radius for her business. If someone at her company reported her missing, this could be really serious."

"Thanks for explaining our job to us, Mr. Tang. Now tell us about the emails you've been sending her."

"What about them?"

"You remember what you wrote?"

"I wrote her lots of things."

"You wrote her all the time, wouldn't you say?"

"I probably wrote to her most days."

"Try every day, Mr. Tang. Two or three times a day, *every* day."

"If you already know that, why ask?"

"It's how we roll. So what did you write about?"

Bobby frowns. "You've obviously read them."

"We'd like to hear it from you."

He shrugs. "I wrote lots of things. Mainly that I loved her, missed her, and wanted her to come back to me."

"And how did she respond?"

Bobby lowers his head. "She didn't."

"You sent two or three emails a day to a wife who never responded." He turns to his partner. "That sound like stalking to you?"

"She's my *wife*," Bobby says. "And anyway, she never asked me to stop emailing her. If she *had*, I would've."

"You wrote to her every day for eight weeks. Never missed a day."

Detective King says, "Until Wednesday. For some reason you suddenly stopped writing to her on Wednesday, and haven't written since."

"I've been busy."

"*Have* you now!"

Brewer takes over: "Your last email to Megan was Wednesday night. Next day she goes missing. You see our problem, don't you?"

Bobby frowns. "Not really."

"We'd like you to come to the station with us, answer a few questions."

Mr. Witt says, "My client has given you his answer. He has no knowledge of his wife's disappearance. Unless you're planning to charge him with a crime, I suggest you leave."

"Is there a reason you're afraid to come downtown?"

"Yes," Mr. Witt says.

The detectives look at each other. Brewer says, "And what is that reason?"

"My wife is hungry."

"Where is she?"

"In a secluded cottage, chained to a wall."

Brewer laughs. "Then perhaps you should fetch her a sandwich. In the meantime, Mr. Tang can come to the station with us. Don't worry, we'll take good care of hm."

Mr. Witt shrugs. "Sounds good to me. What do *you* think, Bobby?"

Chapter 20

BOBBY SAYS, "I'd rather stay here."

Mr. Witt says, "Sorry boys, you heard my client. He'd rather stay here."

Detective King turns to Bobby and tries, unsuccessfully, to force a smile. "I'm afraid we'll have to insist you come to our interrogation room. Now."

Mr. Witt says, "So you can record his answers? I think not. Unless you're charging him with a crime. Are you?"

"Not yet. But we have the right to bring him in, and you know it."

"I do. But if you take him to the station I'll instruct him not to answer any questions."

"And if we question him here?"

Mr. Witt looks Brewer in the eye. "Is this visit part of an official investigation?"

Brewer and King look at each other a moment, then Brewer says, "I'm not sure how to answer that."

Mr. Witt says, "The answer that will give you full, immediate cooperation is 'No, Mr. Witt, this is just an informal conversation.'"

"No, Mr. Witt," Brewer says. "This is just an informal conversation."

"Very well. In that case I'm happy to let him speak to you."

Brewer says, "Thank you." He looks at Bobby. "Mr. Tang?"

"Yes?"

Mr. Witt says, "Call him Bobby, since we're being so informal."

"Fine. Bobby, we'd like you to go on the record as to the last time you saw Megan."

Mr. Witt laughs. "Did you just ask him to go on the record?"

"Sorry. Force of habit."

Mr. Witt says, "Bobby, I'm going to instruct you not to answer the detective's question. However, you can tell *me* the last time you remember seeing Megan. If they happen to overhear us talking there are a number of legal options available to us."

Bobby says, "I saw her about eight weeks ago."

"Do you remember the exact date? Or the occasion?"

"It was the first week of July. We were at her attorney's office, working out the divorce agreement."

Brewer says, "And she gave you the house, the furniture, and the car? In advance of the divorce?"

"That's right."

"Did it strike you as odd she gave you virtually *all* the marital assets?"

"No."

"Why not?"

"Six months ago Megan and I both had good jobs, but we were spending all we earned. Then I lost my job. Megan became very concerned, so I reassured her I had put money away for years as a safeguard."

"And had you?"

"No."

"That was dumb."

Bobby nods. "In retrospect, yeah. But at the time it made sense. I had several job offers over the years and figured someone would snap me up pretty quick." He pauses, caught up in the memory. Then says, "Funny thing about being a mid-level executive: the competition wanted me right up to the moment I was fired."

Brewer says, "That's a sad tale, but you've told us nothing useful. We were discussing the divorce agreement."

Mr. Witt says, "He's trying to establish motive, Bobby. See if you can help him out."

The detectives look at Mr. Witt with gaping jaws.

Mr. Witt laughs. "What, you've never heard an attorney ask his client to help provide a motive for a possible crime?"

Unable to speak, Brewer simply shakes his head.

Bobby says, "While searching for work I borrowed against the house and maxed out our credit cards. Then our world went to shit. We couldn't sell the house because we owed more than it was worth. I finally came clean with Megan and told her how bad things were."

"What did you tell her?"

"That I was planning to file for bankruptcy."

"How did she take it?"

"Not well. She knew everything that happened was my fault. She had a good job, good credit, and didn't want me taking her down. She wanted to transfer all the assets to me so the creditors would have no legal claim against her."

"And in return?"

"I agreed not to file bankruptcy until six months after we were divorced."

"How did you plan to stay afloat during that time?"

"Megan worked out a deal with her company. They gave her an advance against future earnings and converted her accrued sick and vacation days into cash. You know what she did with that money?"

"Tell us."

"She gave it to me. Every last penny."

"Mighty big of her."

"I think so."

"What else did you agree to in the settlement?"

"I agreed not to contest any income she earned during the time we were married."

"Did she specify which income that applied to?"

"All income, from any source."

The detectives look at each other. King says, "I bet you regret that *now!*"

"Why?"

King laughs. "He doesn't know!"

Brewer says, "Un-fucking believable!"

Bobby says, "Look, this was a really hard time for Megan. I was trying to be as understanding as possible."

"Tell us about it."

"We were in the middle of a financial crisis, about to lose everything. Just when we thought things couldn't get any worse, her sister disappeared."

"You're talking about Faith Stallone?"

"That's right."

"Did you and Megan address Faith's estate in your divorce agreement?"

"I agreed not to contest any assets Megan might inherit."

"Why?"

"I didn't feel entitled to her sister's money. And anyway, she and Jake lived a lavish lifestyle. They were living beyond their means same as we were. I certainly didn't want to inherit *their* debt, along with ours."

"*Was* there an inheritance?"

"Not yet, far as I know."

"Faith disappeared two months ago, and now her sister Megan. Does that strike you as a coincidence?"

Bobby says nothing.

Brewer asks, "Have you heard from Faith since her disappearance?"

"No."

"Do you know if she contacted Megan?"

"Not to my knowledge. But you'd know better than me. Your people have interviewed Megan a dozen times."

"Mr. Witt says, "What's the current status on the disappearance?"

Brewer says, "The investigation's ongoing."

Mr. Witt says, "I was out of town when all this took place, but obviously it was in the news. Faith and her husband Jake were linked somehow to the Ryan Decker terrorist attack, correct?"

"That hasn't been proven."

Bobby says, "Jake was having an affair with a woman named Lemon Fister."

Brewer says, "It gets better. Faith and Lemon Fister's husband, Milo, disappeared the day after their spouses were murdered."

Detective King says, "It's a crazy case. Shortly after Faith and Milo disappeared, Milo's body was found in a ditch near Raleigh-Durham International. He'd been stabbed to death."

Mr. Witt says, "Who murdered Lemon and Jake?"

"They were blown to hell during the Ryan Decker terrorist attack."

"They were in one of the houses Decker bombed?"

Brewer nods. "Lemon was entertaining Jake in her home when the attack went down. They probably came and went at the same time."

Bobby says, "The day after the bombing Milo and Faith disappeared."

Mr. Witt says, "Did they run off together, or were they kidnapped?"

Brewer says, "We're not sure. Our working theory is Faith kidnapped and murdered Milo." He turns to Bobby and asks, "How wealthy were the Stallones?"

"I'm not sure. But they lived large."

Detective King says, "Tell us about Carl Roemer."

"Who?"

"Carl Roemer."

"I don't know him. Who is he?"

"Local attorney."

"Sorry. Don't know him."

"Would you be willing to take a polygraph on that?"

Bobby looks at Mr. Witt, then says, "Okay. If you need me to."

Brewer says, "We appreciate your cooperation. He takes out a pad and pen and says, "Can you give me a list of the men Megan has been dating?"

"She hasn't been dating anyone."

King laughs. "Be serious."

"I *am* being serious."

Brewer says, "What if I told you I have certain proof of at least one steady boyfriend?"

"I'd be extremely disappointed."

"Would you be angry?"

Mr. Witt says, "Bobby? Don't answer that."

Bobby says, "What's the guy's name?"

Brewer hesitates, then says, "I think we'd better keep that confidential for now."

"Is it the attorney you just asked me about? Carl Roemer?"

"Let's talk about the lottery."

"What lottery?"

Chapter 21

DETECTIVE BREWER SAYS, "Has Megan spoken to you about the lottery?"

Bobby says, "There's not much to talk about. She bought tickets from time to time, but never won anything."

"Never?"

"Five or ten bucks, I suppose. Nothing major."

King gives him a long look. Then says, "Tell us about your off-shore bank account."

"*What?*"

Brewer says, "In the Bahamas."

Bobby laughs derisively. "I'm unemployed. I barely have a *local* bank account!"

"I'd like you on the record saying you don't have an off-shore bank account."

Bobby looks at Mr. Witt. To everyone's surprise, he motions Bobby to answer the question.

"Fine," Bobby says. "I don't have an off-shore bank account."

"Know anyone who does?"

"I don't travel in those circles."

"For the record, please?"

"No. I don't know anyone who has an off-shore bank account. Why do you ask?"

"This past Friday Megan wired $10 million to an off-shore account in the Bahamas."

"You said she disappeared on Thursday. How could she wire money on Friday?"

"That's what we'd like to know."

"You're way off base," Bobby says.

"Why's that?"

"The whole notion's ridiculous! Where would Megan get $10 million to wire in the first place?"

"She won the lottery."

"Bullshit."

"You honestly didn't know?"

"You've obviously made a mistake. She would have told me if she won the lottery. She knows I'm having financial trouble. She would have helped me."

"You'd *think* so, wouldn't you?"

"I know so."

"She wasn't talking to you at all, though, was she?"

The detectives go quiet, allowing Bobby to think about it. The longer he thinks, the redder his face gets. Finally he asks, "How much did she win?"

"Don't know. But the cash option was $107 million. After taxes the total deposited to her account was $57,780,000, in rounded numbers."

"That's bullshit."

Brewer says, "She held the ticket two weeks before cashing it."

"So?"

"She shafted you. She bought the ticket, won the lottery, decided not to share it with you. To keep you from claiming half the money, she asked for a quick divorce. Gave you all the marital assets and talked you into signing away your rights to any assets she received during the marriage. Including the $107 million she won from the lottery."

King says, "Feel like a sap, Bobby?"

Brewer says, "She blamed the divorce on your financial trouble and her sister's disappearance, but it was really about the lottery ticket."

Bobby stares straight ahead, says nothing.

Brewer says, "You were married how long?"

Bobby fails to respond, so Brewer repeats the question.

Bobby says, "Six years, give or take."

"She must have *hated* your ass!"

Bobby says, "Assuming all this is true, why would she wire money to an off-shore account?"

"We were hoping you could tell us."

"Well, like I said, I don't know anything about it."

"So you say."

"You don't believe me?"

"We'd like to," Brewer says, "but this is a lot of money. Our working theory is you found out about the lottery and demanded half the money. She refused, so you kidnapped her and forced her to wire $10 million to your off-shore account."

"That's crazy. Wait. Why just $10 million?"

"Maybe you're not greedy. Or maybe you made her wire money to other places we don't know about."

Bobby frowns. "In your theory, what did I do with Megan after she wired the money?"

"Again, we were hoping you'd tell us."

"You mentioned a guy named Carl something-or-other. Is he the one who reported her missing?"

"We'll ask the questions, if you don't mind, starting with this: when are you available to take the lie detector test?"

"About the off-shore bank account? Anytime you like."

"We'd have other questions."

"Like what?"

Brewer says, "Let's cut to the chase: are there any questions you'd refuse to answer?"

"Yes."

"Such as?"

"I'm not going to discuss where I've been or what I've been doing for the past few days."

The detectives look at each other incredulously, then back at Bobby. Brewer says, "Why not?"

"It's personal."

"You're refusing to tell us what you've been doing since Friday?"

"That's right."

Brewer gives him the cop stare for a full minute before saying, "We'd still like to do a polygraph on the questions you're willing to answer."

"When?"

"As soon as we can set it up."

Chapter 22

WHEN THE DETECTIVES are gone, Mr. Witt says, "You lied to me."

"About what?"

"You said Megan wasn't dating."

"She's not."

"You're absolutely certain?"

Bobby nods, but not convincingly.

Mr. Witt says, "In my experience, if police detectives claim proof of a boyfriend, it's usually true."

"You promised you'd talk her into coming back to me."

"I did. But I was unaware she'd been kidnapped."

"She hasn't been kidnapped."

Mr. Witt gives him a curious look. "You know where she is?"

He nods. "Bahamas."

"You know this for a fact?"

"No, but I'd be willing to bet all the money you owe me."

"Why the Bahamas?"

"Megan loves it there. Think about it. The detective said she went missing on Thursday. Then she wired $10 million to an offshore account on Friday. In the Bahamas. But they refused to tell us who reported her missing."

"What's *your* theory?"

"I think her bank probably reported the wire transfer, and the detectives made up the kidnapping story to scare me."

"Why would that scare *you*?"

"It doesn't. But if I *had* kidnapped her, it'd scare the shit out of me."

"I don't want you to think I'm siding with the detectives, but forgetting the possible kidnapping, I can't help but notice you don't seem very upset your wife cheated you out of $57 million."

He shrugs. "I have faith in Megan."

"What's that mean?"

"My guess is she's planning a surprise for me."

"What kind of surprise?"

Bobby smiles. "I think she's going to give our marriage another shot. I think she's planning to move there, buy a gorgeous house on the beach, then call me to come live with her."

"Can you possibly be this naïve?"

"Like I say, I have faith in Megan."

"How do you explain the fact she hasn't responded to your emails?"

"She needed time to deal with her sister's situation. And it obviously took weeks to work out the lottery payment. Think about it from her point of view. How much bigger will the surprise be if she calls me out of the blue to say she's won the lottery, she's taking me back, and we're going to live in the Bahamas?"

"It'd surprise the shit out of *me*, at least," Mr. Witt says. Then adds, "But if you honestly believe that, why didn't you tell the detectives?"

"I didn't want to spoil Megan's surprise."

Mr. Witt frowns deeply.

"What's wrong?"

"I'm getting a bad feeling."

"About what?"

"If the detectives are right, and Megan turns up dead, you could have a problem."

"That's crazy. Who'd kill Megan?"

"*You*, according to the detectives. And how can you blame them? After writing to her several times a day for eight weeks, you stop the night before she goes *missing*?"

Bobby considers it. "You said you'd protect me."

"I will. But I need to know everything you know."

"I've told you everything I know."

"You must have known she won the lottery."

He shakes his head.

"I find that virtually impossible to believe."

"I swear on my life!"

"The problem I'm having, you didn't seem very surprised."

"Neither did you."

"Well *that's* obviously not true. I was so shocked I let you keep talking when I should have made you shut up."

"Good to hear in case I decide to sue you for malpractice."

Mr. Witt laughs. "You can sue my wife for having sugar tits, but you won't win a judgment."

"What's that supposed to mean?"

"I'm not an attorney, Bobby. I only told the detectives that to keep them from taking advantage of you."

"Your wife has sugar tits? What's that, like diabetes or something?"

"Let's not get sidetracked. You're probably right about Megan being in the Bahamas. It makes sense she'd wire money there if she's planning to buy a place. It also makes sense she'd use a numbered account instead of her name. For security purposes."

"There's more," Bobby says. "I recently learned Megan set up an annuity for my parents."

"How much?"

"I don't know. A lot. But it's further proof she still cares for me."

"Just to be clear, you're not concerned about a possible boyfriend."

He shakes his head. "No. My only concern is the guy I sprayed in the bathroom."

"Don't be. They can't tie it to you."

"You're sure?"

"You didn't know the guy, right?"

"Right."

"Then there's no reason to suspect you. Plus, you were here when the detectives arrived, so they're your alibi."

"Good. So what happens now?"

Mr. Witt smiles. "We continue on as though nothing happened. Tonight you'll earn your next bonus."

"I think I'm going to stop."

"Why?"

"There's too much going on. The detectives are probably watching my house right now."

"No they're not. You're cooperating. You agreed to take a polygraph as soon as they can set it up. If Megan's safe in the Bahamas, or anywhere else in the world, there's no crime. If she *has* been kidnapped, and you know nothing about it, you'll pass the polygraph."

"What if they follow me?"

"This isn't the movies."

"I know, but still. I think I'm going to sit this one out."

"These two are a package deal."

"Are you refusing to pay me?"

"For what you did yesterday? No problem, check's in the mail. But if you want payment for what happened today in the men's room you'll have to follow through with the girls tonight and tomorrow. And by the way, that's a *reward*, not a burden!"

Bobby stares straight ahead.

Mr. Witt says, "You wanted extra work, I got you sixty grand. You did the hard one. Now you're essentially being paid sixty grand to have the best sex of your life!"

Bobby sighs. "When do you need an answer?"

"Right now. Or we're done."

"I suppose you could blackmail me. About the bathroom guy."

"That would be pretty stupid, since I masterminded it."

"But I carried it out."

"Two words: Charles Manson."

"What do you mean?"

"He was the mastermind, not the killer. He wasn't even there. But he's still in prison."

"Good point."

"We're on the same team, Bobby. We're in this together."

"What if the detectives come back?"

"If you're still on my team, I'll keep you safe. You have my word."

"Okay."

"Okay? What's that mean? You're on the team? You'll do the challenges?"

Bobby nods.

"Excellent. I'll see you at 7 p.m."

"Which one will I be with tonight?"

"You can't know. By the way, you'll be hooded and handcuffed to insure a fair contest. And Bobby?"

"Yeah?"

"Get excited, will you? Two hot girls are highly motivated to give you the best they've got. This is something you'll remember the rest of your life! You're a lucky man. Act like it."

"I'll try." He pauses, then says, "You're sure he's dead? The guy in the bathroom?"

"Positive."

Chapter 23

ANDREW WITT WASN'T lying about his wife being in a secluded cottage, chained to the wall. As he pulls off the two-lane onto the dirt road he lowers his window and drives slowly, listening for her screams. He shouldn't be able to hear any, even when he gets to the porch, since the basement is so thoroughly soundproofed. Then again, as his old math teacher used to say, it's always a good idea to check your work before turning it in.

Andrew enters the main room carrying the bag that contains Betty's lunch. Places it on the floor, slides the sofa out of the way; lifts the trap door that leads to the basement, enters, and locks it from the basement side. Then descends the stairs, unlocks the steel door at the bottom, enters the room, locks the steel door behind him.

"Hi Mommy!" he says, brightly.

"Fuck you!" Betty says.

"He glances at the blinking light on the monitor he keeps out of her reach and says, "Good. You got my message. Sorry I'm late, but I brought you a nice, healthy lunch."

She says nothing, so he adds, "I went through the cafeteria line. Got all your favorites."

He walks to the plastic children's table, places the container and plastic utensils on it, and motions her to sit on the little plastic stool. Betty's bindings allow her a limited range of access that extends to the table, the mattress, the camper's toilet, and the lemons and bottled waters stacked against the wall. Her only source of entertainment is the cable TV. She can't reach the TV itself, but controls it with the remote.

Mr. Witt has his own remote.

The area surrounding the cottage is monitored by eight infrared cameras. If something or someone enters the area his phone makes a sound. He can click a button and access the visual. He can even converse with the intruder if he wishes.

He can also keep an eye on Betty and talk to her whenever it suits him.

So far, no one has entered the area except him. Of course, Betty's only been his prisoner a few weeks. Ever since...

"I ran into one of our neighbors earlier today," Mr. Witt says. Noting the flicker of interest in his wife's eyes he says, "Nat Bailey." He points at the table. "Food's getting cold."

She approaches the table, sits on the plastic chair. Mr. Witt says, "Nat said to give you his best. Said he hasn't seen you at the gym or walking around the neighborhood lately."

She says nothing, so he stares at her, watches her eat.

Betty's a mess.

Her hair's matted. She's dirty, pale, disheveled, and her BO smells like man ass at the homeless shelter. Her expression, like her attitude, is one of defeat. After weeks of screaming, crying, pleading, she's come to the conclusion she's never going to get out of here alive.

She's right.

Mr. Witt waits for her to finish eating, then hands her a paper towel and bags the refuse, making sure to collect the plastic knife, fork, and spoon so she can't use them to cut herself or fashion some sort of crude weapon to use against him.

Not that it would help.

Mr. Witt couldn't set her free if he wanted to, unless he brings bolt cutters. On day one of her captivity he made sure she saw him destroy the key to the padlocks that should keep her chained for the rest of her life. He explained that *he*—and *only* he—was the "key" to her survival. That even if she somehow managed to kill him, she'd never be able to escape without outside help. And her only chance for that would be if she could access his cell phone. But since he uses a 10-digit security code the likelihood of her making a phone call virtually zero.

"So you may as well cooperate," he said that first day.

To Mr. Witt, *cooperate* meant more than having his way with her sexually.

125

"You really should take regular sponge baths," he says. "This morning I noticed two boils on your ass. They're only going to get worse."

"Fuck you!" she says.

Fuck, and *you*, and *I*, and *hate*, and *bastard*—and their derivatives—are the five words that make up 90% of her conversational output. Her biggest sentence this week has been "I hate you, you fucking bastard!"

He approaches her, makes her face the wall. Removes three twist-ties from his pocket and uses them to bind her wrists behind her back. Then he gets the bar of soap, roll of paper towels, and several bottles of water she should have used today. Pulls her sweat pants down to the metal cuffs to which her ankles are chained, bends her over; carefully cleans her up. Turns her around, soaps her crotch. Rinses it, pats it dry. Then pulls her pants back up to her waist, unbuttons her blouse, and carefully washes—then dries—her breasts. He gets a lemon from the pile, rips it in half, rubs her nipples with them. Then eases her onto the bed, walks across the room to the giant clothes trunk, strips, puts on an adult diaper, gets down on his hands and knees, crawls over to the bed and says, "Mommy, I'm hungry. Feed me, Mommy."

"Fuck you!"

He works his way to her breast and starts sucking. It takes a moment, but the milk finally spurts.

"I *hate* you!" Betty screams.

"I *love you*, Mommy," Mr. Witt coos happily.

He sucks each breast for five minutes, then licks them clean. He'd like to fall asleep with his head in her lap, the way he used to when they first started dating, but she's wise to that move. If he tries, she'll spit his face. If he turns his face into her crotch she'll try to piss him.

It's less pleasant than it sounds, since for some reason "capture" piss smells a lot like asparagus piss.

He lies beside her, fondling and suckling her breasts till she hears him make the dreaded sound.

"Mommy?" he says. "I made a doody. Time to clean me up, Mommy."

This part always goes badly.

First, he cuts the twist ties. Though her wrists are still chained, she can move them around. In an ideal world, she'd wipe his ass and sponge him as carefully as he cleaned her.

But this isn't an ideal world, and Andrew knows what's coming.

He angles his butt to give her the proper access on the chance she's keen to clean it, but as usual, she's in a rotten mood. She grabs his shit and tries to smear it in his hair. He rolls away just in time and says, "We'll try again tomorrow, Mommy."

She flings the shit at him and yells, "I hate you! I *hate* you!"

He sighs. "Try to get some rest, Mommy."

He uses her wet wipes to clean himself up. As he's getting dressed, his phone vibrates. He checks caller ID, sees Bobby Tang's name. He can't answer it because Betty will probably start shrieking that she's being held prisoner. He finishes dressing, then reverses the process that allowed him access to the basement. When he gets to his car he calls Bobby back and says, "What's up?"

Bobby says, "I need you to come to my house."

"When?"

"Now. Right now!"

"What's wrong?"

"The detectives are back. They're going to arrest me on suspicion of murder."

"No they're not. Wait. *Who's* murder?"

"Some guy named Nat Bailey."

"Let me speak to Detective Brewer."

Brewer takes the phone and says, "Hello again, counselor. Imagine our surprise just moments ago when we got the call that Nat Bailey was found dead in a public men's room."

"Who's Nat Bailey, and how's he connected to Bobby Tang?"

"Nat's the guy Megan's been fucking for the past two months."

"Put Bobby on the phone."

Bobby says, "You heard that?"

"Yeah. What are the odds?"

"That's all you've got to say about it?" Bobby says, panic-stricken.

"Tell Brewer I'll be there in 20 minutes. In the meantime, say nothing."

"*Hurry!*"

Chapter 24

ON THE WAY to Bobby's, Mr. Witt takes a moment to consider how well his life has turned out. His relationship with Betty isn't perfect, but things might improve now that Nat Bailey's out of the picture.

Despite what Detective Brewer said, Nat Bailey wasn't fucking Bobby's wife.

He was fucking Andrew Witt's wife, Betty.

Had *been* fucking her for the past six months!

Killing Nat wasn't part of the plan, but he had to die, and Mr. Witt wanted to personally kill him. Nevertheless, it can't hurt to let Bobby believe *he* murdered Nat.

Mr. Witt learned about Betty's affair through Nat's co-worker, Carl Roemer. Carl told a guy who told a guy, and that guy told Mr. Witt. The guy also said Nat was a meth junkie, so Mr. Witt tracked down his dealer, Seppi, and paid him to cut off all contact with Nat. Then Mr. Witt paid Carl to change the rumor he'd been spreading. From that point on, the woman Nat was having an affair with became Megan Tang, not Betty Witt. Mr. Witt began posing as Nat's new dealer, and all correspondence between them was by text. Nat immediately asked his new dealer for heroin, and Mr. Witt said to give him two weeks.

"When I get the product," he said, "I'll text you the single letter H. When you see that, stop what you're doing and go straight to the lobby bathroom of the Dorfman-Beck building. Step up to the urinal. My associate will enter the bathroom and spritz some water in your face. Don't be alarmed, it's just water. But he thinks it's poison, so I want you to fall to the floor and pretend you're dying. The poison, DMSO, should take 38 seconds to kill you, so lie there till I come in. When I do, I'll have your product. And by the way, your first taste is on the house."

The rest, as they say....

Mr. Witt never confronted Betty about the affair. It bothered the hell out of him that he was unable to detect any hint of infidelity in his wife's voice or actions. It's a hard thing to come to grips with, finding out how good a liar your wife is, and over time, it ate him up. He finally snapped, and as a result, she's now residing at the cottage.

When Nat's death makes the newspaper he'll bring her one and watch her face as she reads that her lover is dead. Perhaps she'll seek comfort in Andrew's arms. Perhaps he'll ask why she's so upset over the death of a casual neighbor. Whatever happens, it'll be fun to see how she responds. If things go badly, and she angers him, Andrew will show her the photos he took of Nat's body and private parts.

Then again, he might be kidding himself. It's possible Betty already suspects he knows about her affair. During the first days of her captivity she asked him a thousand times why he was doing this to her, and though he never responded, she must suspect it's either or both of two things: her affair, or because she refused to be his milk whore.

No matter. Andrew's living the good life. He's wealthy, about to become wealthier, and happier than at any time during his eight-year marriage. That's because—shockingly—not once during their marriage has Betty expressed the slightest interest in breastfeeding him. Nor did she even think it was possible that a non-pregnant woman could nurse. She'd never heard of induced lactation, or domperidone, the gastrointestinal medication whose side effect stimulates the release of prolactin so effectively it can actually cause men to lactate.

He chuckles, remembering how Betty thought he was giving her Dom Perignon pills for her nausea. The pills were so effective she willingly took them, completely unaware her breasts were being prepped for lactation. Mr. Witt's original plan had been to stimulate her breasts with massage, then compression, and in the final stages, with an electric breast pump every three hours for two weeks. By then she'd be able to breastfeed half of Nashville!

Betty enjoyed the massages, but the compression phase was so painful she accused him of assault. She became furious and barred him from ever touching her boobs again.

He was positively stunned by her reaction. "I'd rather cut my dick off!" he said.

When he tried to explain the true purpose for his actions she called him a creepy, degenerate pervert. When she learned domperidone was a prescription drug, she threatened to report him to the police. He couldn't have that, and was already pissed off about the affair, so he kidnapped her and brought her to his cottage in the woods.

Andrew knows what his wife is thinking: she's never been pregnant, so her milk should dry up soon.

Not true.

Betty's only 38, and if properly handled, should be able to lactate for another 40 years. After all, legendary wet-nurse Judith Waterford was still producing breast milk at the age of 81, and that was more than 180 years ago!

Mr. Witt isn't greedy. He'll settle for a daily fuck and a half-pint of breast milk. If Betty wants to treat him like shit he can deal with it because he's got enough love for both of them. When she gets particularly surly, he'll give her an injection, put her to sleep, and bring out the breast pump.

Only problem is, she's always surly.

Betty might disagree, but from Andrew's point of view the marriage is solid, the breast milk is liquid, and the always-available sex is icing on the cake. He lives for the weekends, when he has more time to devote to the process. That's when he gets to enjoy Betty's hindmilk, which is vastly preferable to her foremilk, which is produced at the beginning of each feeding. The foremilk is watery, weak-flavored, and altogether unsatisfying. By contrast, the hindmilk comes from the nearly empty breast. It's creamy, white, full-flavored, and yummy.

But try explaining that to Bitch Betty.

Chapter 25

BOBBY TANG'S AS nervous as a celebrity's wrinkle in a Botox factory. He says, "They think I killed Megan's lover."

"That's absurd," Mr. Witt says.

"Is it?" Detective Brewer says.

"It must be. I just said it was."

"You won't be laughing for long, asshole."

"I'm not laughing now. This whole scenario is bullshit. If you had any intention of arresting Bobby, you'd have already done so, and we'd be having this discussion at the police station instead of Bobby's living room. You're here because you've got questions, not answers."

Brewer frowns. "The answers he gives will determine what happens next."

"Good. So ask your questions already, and let Bobby get back to his life."

Bobby's amazed at Mr. Witt's level of confidence. The moment he arrived, the dynamic changed. He's completely in charge. Bobby feels empowered. When Brewer says, "Tell us about Nat Bailey," Bobby says, "Never heard of him."

"You're sure about that?"

"Positive."

"And yet he's dead."

Mr. Witt says, "Ask Bobby about Abraham Lincoln. He's dead too."

Bobby coughs out a laugh that's 90% relief.

Brewer says, "Very well. Bobby?"

"Yeah?"

"Has Abraham Lincoln been fucking your wife for the past two months?"

"I'll say no."

"Well Nat Bailey was."

"I seriously doubt Megan has been with anyone since breaking up with me. But even if I'm wrong about that, I've *still* never heard of Nat Baily, and that's the truth."

"We'll see. But the indisputable fact is your wife, Megan Tang, has been dating Nat Bailey for at least two months, and possibly longer. Shortly after two this afternoon Mr. Bailey was seen heading toward the Dorfman-Beck building. His body was discovered in the men's room 15 minutes later."

Mr. Witt smiles and says, "You haven't said how Mr. Bailey died, but your demeanor suggests foul play. If you're suggesting Bobby needs an alibi for Mr. Bailey's demise, I'll remind you I arrived here before three o'clock today, and when I did, you and Detective King were already here. I assume your records reflect that."

"The Dorfman-Beck is a 12-minute drive from Mr. Tang's house."

"So?"

"We checked our records and concluded Bobby had time to kill Mr. Bailey and return here prior to our arrival at 2:50 p.m."

"That's an awfully tight window of opportunity to commit a murder."

"But certainly possible. And he had the motive."

"Oldest one in the book," Detective King adds.

"You're suggesting Bobby somehow managed to lure Mr. Bailey out of his office at the precise time he needed to in order to kill him and get back to his house before you showed up?"

"That's right."

"Then I've got a question for you, Detective. How could Bobby possibly know you were planning to come to his house at 2:50 p.m. today? Had you given him any prior notice?"

The detectives look at each other.

Mr. Witt says, "How about we ask Bobby where he was at 2:00 p.m. today."

Brewer says, "Okay by me. On the record, Mr. Tang, where were you at 2:00 p.m. today?"

While the detectives stare at Bobby, Mr. Witt mouths the word, *here.*

"I was here," Bobby says.

"And your housekeeper?"

"Sir?"

"Was she here also?"

Mr. Witt says, "Let's ask her."

Brewer says, "Detective King, please remain here with Mr. Tang while his attorney and I talk to his housekeeper."

"No need to separate them," Mr. Witt says. "Is she still here Bobby?"

He nods. "She's in the kitchen."

"Lead the way."

As it turns out, she's in the laundry room. "Miss Tate?" Brewer says.

"Yes sir?"

"What time did you arrive here today?"

She looks at Bobby. Brewer says, "Keep your eyes on me, please, and answer the question."

"About 8:30 this morning."

"And was Mr. Tang here when you arrived?"

"Yes sir."

"And what time did he leave the house?"

"Um...you mean today?"

"Yes."

"He hasn't."

"Hasn't left the house?"

"No sir."

Bobby and Mr. Witt exchange a glance. They can't believe their ears.

Brewer says, "He's been here the entire day? Since 8:30 a.m.? You're certain?"

"Yes sir."

"Is that normal?"

"Lately, yes."

"And why is that?"

"He's unemployed."

Mr. Witt says, "You have your answer, Detective. Need I remind you it was unrehearsed?"

"I'll decide when we're done here." He gives Kennon the hard stare and says, "This isn't a casual conversation, Miss Tate. We're in the first stage of a murder investigation, and your responses are being documented for the record. If it turns out you're lying, you could do serious jail time." He softens his voice and adds, "You're too pretty to go to prison, Kennon. You can't begin to fathom what they'll do to you there."

"I'm sure you're right, Detective. I can't begin to fathom it. Nor will I need to experience it, since I'm not a liar. Mr. Tang has been here all day. He hasn't left the house."

Brewer scowls. "*For the record, Miss Tate...*"

"Yes sir?"

"Were you present in this house between the hours two and three o'clock today?"

"Yes sir. I've been here all day."

"Perhaps you were busy in another part of the house and didn't see Mr. Tang leave the property."

"He didn't leave the property today. I'm certain."

Detective King sets his jaw. "How can you be so sure?"

"The trash people came at 1:45."

"So?"

"After they picked up the trash, I put the cans back in the garage."

"So?"

"Mr. Tang's car was in the garage."

"Perhaps he left shortly after."

"He couldn't have."

"Why not?"

"He had a flat tire."

"*What?*"

Mr. Witt does a double take, and he's not alone. For a moment, no one speaks. Then Detective Brewer says, "He had a flat tire?"

"Yes sir."

"And did he fix it?"

"No sir. It's still flat."

Detective Brewer shakes his head and mutters something. Then asks, "Does he have any other cars?"

"No sir."

"Maybe he borrowed yours."

"I don't own a car."

"How did you get to work?"

"My boyfriend dropped me off."

"What's his name?"

She looks at Mr. Witt, who says, "You don't have to answer. It's completely irrelevant."

Brewer says, "We'll let the jury decide what's relevant."

"I agree. Kennon, tell the jury, not us. In the meantime, Detective, shouldn't we check to see if Bobby's tire is flat?"

Chapter 26

THE GROUP HEADS to the garage and find Bobby's rear tire as flat as the economic recovery. And no one seems more surprised than Bobby.

Detective King says, "Why haven't you fixed it?"

Bobby shrugs. "It's not like I had to *be* anywhere. I lost my job, remember?"

"Did you know your tire was flat before Miss Tate mentioned it?"

"I noticed it last night, when I set the trash cans out."

"And it's been flat the whole time?"

"Does it *look* fixed?" Mr. Witt says.

Brewer looks at Kennon. "Thank you, Miss Tate. You've been a big help."

"You're welcome." She turns, goes back in the house.

"Are we done here?" Mr. Witt says.

Brewer's eyes find Bobby's. "Did you pay someone to kill Nat Bailey?"

"I'm broke, remember?"

"Answer the question, please."

"No. I didn't pay anyone to kill Nat Bailey. I never even heard of the guy before you said his name."

"So you say. I assume you're still up for the polygraph?"

"Uh...."

Mr. Witt says, "If after all this you still want one, my client will take it. He's got nothing to hide."

Brewer eyes Bobby carefully. "We'll ask if you've ever met Nat Bailey."

Bobby looks uneasy.

Detective King joins in. "If you ever met him, or knew he was fucking your wife, it'll show up on the polygraph."

"He understands that," Mr. Witt says.

Bobby holds it together till the detectives leave. Then he falls apart. "I'm going to prison!" he laments. "I *told* you we'd get caught!"

"I've got to admit that was bad luck."

"Bad luck? You think? Nothing ever works for me. I swear, if you locked me in a barrel of tits I'd come out sucking my thumb."

Mr. Witt says, "Relax. You never met the guy."

"Of course I did. I *killed* him."

"Maybe so, but you didn't actually *meet* him. Remind yourself of that when they ask the question."

"And when they ask if I killed him?"

"Did you see him die?"

"No."

"Remind yourself of *that* when they ask the question."

"Will that work?"

"Doesn't matter. They can't use the results against you."

"Then why take it?"

"It gives you credibility. But again, there's nothing to worry about, because if you perform the task tonight and tomorrow, I'll teach you how to beat the polygraph."

"You've done it?"

"Yes. And you can, too."

"How?"

"The short answer? It's not a lie if you believe it."

"What does that mean?"

"I'll explain when the time comes. As a backup, I'll teach you how to flub the control questions. The test results will be so skewed they won't know what to do with them."

Bobby shakes his head back and forth. "I can't *believe* this shit! It makes no *sense!*"

"What doesn't?"

"The first guy who took a piss happened to be Megan's *boyfriend?* How's that possible?"

"I've been asking myself that same question since Brewer said it. Know what I've come up with?"

"What?"

"You knew."

"What?"

"You knew Nat Bailey was fucking your wife."

Bobby's jaw drops. "Are you *insane?*"

"It's the only thing that makes sense."

"If *you* don't believe me I'm up the fucking creek."

Mr. Witt shrugs. "It doesn't matter what I think."

"It does to me. I can't pass the polygraph without your help."

"Perhaps not. But there's another possibility I haven't mentioned."

"What's that?"

"Don't take the test."

"What do you mean?"

"I'll call Detective Brewer and tell him you changed your mind."

"He'll be more suspicious than ever!"

"Who gives a shit? You're home free."

Bobby looks exasperated. "How do you figure that?"

"Kennon gave you an ironclad alibi. She saved your ass."

Bobby stares at him.

Mr. Witt says, "Why would she do that?"

Bobby turns his palms up. "I have no idea."

"She obviously punctured your tire."

Bobby says nothing, so Mr. Witt says, "She must have done it the minute they showed up. Otherwise, we would've heard air coming out."

Bobby thinks about it a minute. Then says, "What's going on here?"

"What do you mean?"

"Who the fuck *is* she?"

"Who, Kennon?"

"She's working with you, isn't she?"

"She works for *you*, Bobby."

"Is she the movie star? The one I'm supposed to have sex with?"

Mr. Witt throws his head back and roars with laughter. "If *that's* what you think I'm afraid you're going to be terribly disappointed."

Bobby bristles. "Are you claiming you never met her before today?"

Mr. Witt says nothing, just stares at Bobby as if he's seeing him for the first time.

Bobby says, "She's working for you, isn't she?"

"No she's not. And I think you know that. In fact, I think I've seriously underestimated you."

Bobby stares at him blankly.

Mr. Witt says, "I wonder if I was right the first time."

"About what?"

"That you and Kennon are a couple."

"That's ridiculous."

"Is it?"

Bobby frowns. "Now you sound like Brewer."

Mr. Witt clears his throat. "I'm just wondering why you're standing here talking to me instead of asking Kennon what possessed her to puncture your tire and give you an alibi."

"Good point."

They find Kennon standing in the kitchen. Before they have time to speak, she says, "I'll pay for the tire."

The two men look at each other. Mr. Witt chuckles. "*I'll pay for the tire!* And give you a job if you want."

She wrinkles her perfect nose. "No offense, Mr. Witt, but whatever you're involved in would not interest me."

Bobby says, "Why'd you do it?"

"To protect you."

"From what?"

"While you were on the phone I heard the detectives trying to decide if you could have driven here from Candlewood Plaza between 2:20 and 2:45. I knew you could, because you did."

"So you gave me an alibi."

She nods.

"Why?"

"You never tried to hit on me."

Bobby looks confused.

She adds, "I think you're a good person."

Mr. Witt says, "You risked jail time because he never *hit* on you?"

"They thought he murdered a man."

"And?"

"I knew that couldn't possibly be true. But sometimes people wind up in the wrong place at the wrong time."

Bobby says, "If I ask you something, will you promise to answer honestly?"

"I'll try. I mean, I may not *know* the answer."

"You'll know. My question is this: are you working for Mr. Witt in any capacity?"

"*What? Him? Of course* not! Didn't he leave you handcuffed this morning just to *embarrass* me?" She gives him a dirty look. "And didn't he just offer me a *job?*"

"He did. But I thought he might be covering up."

"Covering up what?"

"The fact that you're working for him."

"If I were working for him I wouldn't be *here*, would I?"

"You probably *would* be."

She shakes her head. "Maybe I shouldn't have punctured your tire."

Mr. Witt says, "Long as we're on the subject, what did you use?"

"Ice pick."

Bobby says, "We don't have an ice pick here."

Kennon opens her purse. There are other items in it, but all they see is the ice pick.

Mr. Witt says, "What sort of person carries an ice pick in her purse?"

Kennon looks at Bobby. "Would you like me to change your tire now?"

"No, of course not! I'll do it. And Kennon? Thank you. I can't tell you how much I appreciate you for doing that."

"You *are* innocent, aren't you?"

"Yes, of course."

"Then there's no need to thank me. It just means I did the right thing."

Chapter 27

MEGAN FRY IS healing. The sadistic goon who calls himself Bad Man hasn't beaten her for days. He tortured and beat her continuously from the time of her abduction to 10:00 a.m. Friday, at which point he removed her hood and forced her to call her bank to wire $10 million to a numbered account in the Bahamas. Megan's eyes were so swollen from the beatings she couldn't read the wiring instructions, so Bad Man had to write the account numbers in large print on two sheets of paper. Then he put the hood back on her head and beat her till the bank called her back with additional questions.

"If you screw this up, you die," he warned.

Megan didn't screw up, thank God, and the man rewarded her by only torturing her another six hours. Then he removed her hood and left her alone for the better part of three days. But now a new man has entered the concrete chamber where she's being held captive. He's older, possibly

40, and dressed like an English undertaker. He's holding a cane in one hand, an iPad in the other, and there's a coil of rope around his neck.

He props the cane against the wall and says, "Got a joke for you: A young lady's in a grocery store checkout line. Each time she places an item on the conveyer belt the drunk behind her calls it out: 'Bacon!' he says. 'Eggs...milk...butter.' Then he says, 'You're *single!*' She looks at the items, then at him, and says, 'You're right, I *am* single. But how did you *know?*' He says, "'Cause you're uglier than *shit!*'"

Megan stares at him blankly.

Then he says something that shocks the shit out of her. Shocks her so completely, she asks him to repeat it. So he does:

"I said your husband Bobby sends his regards."

The man moves closer.

"He's doing fine, by the way. I'll show you some pictures to prove it." He tilts the iPad so she can get a better look. "This is Bobby naked, handcuffed to the bed. You probably thought since you didn't want him, no one else would want him either, am I right?"

He advances the slide show. "This is the girl he fucked last night. She's not quite in your league, Megan, but she's certainly doable, don't you think? Now here's the real prize. On your best day you could never look like *this* one. Meet Kennon, the housekeeper." He laughs. "I know, right? *You* hired her! Did you have any idea how incredibly good-looking she was when you chose her? If so, you must have no feelings for Bobby whatsoever." He pauses. "I won't show you what happened next, since I don't wish to make you blush. But let's just say Kennon's the one who removed the cuffs. Are you jealous?"

She shakes her head, no.

"Well, that's a real pity, because even with all this action on the side, Bobby's pining away for you like a whale separated from its calf. But this you already know, since he's begged you to come back a hundred times."

She looks at him but doesn't speak.

He says, "I told you that joke for two reasons. The first is, like the lady at the checkout line, *you* look uglier than shit. Because of the swelling and bruises, of course. And you *smell* like shit, too. He lifts his head and sniffs, as if rating a fine wine. I'm getting a definite feces-urine scent in the room, with a hint of copper from the blood that's been spilled. There's also a delicate undercurrent of rotten eggs which I recognize as the scent of scabs forming on the wounds you've suffered. Of course, I'd be remiss if I failed to mention the strong, musty scent emanating from..." He bends at the waist and lowers his head till his nose is four inches from her lower abdomen. He winces and says, "Well, no need to get personal. But trust me when I say you're due for a shower and change of clothes. What's it been, six days without soap?"

When she fails to answer he says, "The second reason I told you that joke is because it contains an element of surprise. Do you like surprises?"

Megan—still reeling from the revelation that Bobby may have hired these horrible men—says nothing.

"I hope so," the man says, "because I have a surprise for *you.*"

"Sir?"

"You're going to compensate Bobby for fucking him over with your bullshit divorce settlement, and yes, I'm talking about the lottery money."

She waits a moment; then says, "I already wired $10 million on Friday."

"Yes, you did. And now you're going to transfer the rest of the money to your joint account."

"I—"

"Yes?"

"I don't use that account any more. I don't even have the information. The...you know, the numbers? Routing system? ...bank address? ...any of it."

"Not to worry. As it happens, I've got one of your joint account checks right here. You'll call your account manager and transfer every nickel from your personal checking account to your joint account."

Megan's face falls. "*All* of it? *Everything?*"

He shows her a thin smile. "I'm not heartless. I'll let you keep twenty grand. How's that?"

She starts to cry.

He makes no attempt to comfort her, just patiently waits for her to finish.

Eventually she says, "Bobby did this to me?"

"Bobby should ask *you* the same question. Did you *really* do that to him? Walk out on the marriage simply because he lost his job and couldn't pay the bills?"

"There was more to it than—"

"Of course there was. There always is. It's a marriage, after all." He pauses. "Things get tough, tempers flare. But you

149

won the lottery!" He flashes a smile that's all teeth and no conviction. "But instead of calling Bobby to tell him his financial problems were solved, you hired an attorney to cheat him out of the money."

He glares at her a moment, then says, "You know what I'd like to know? What sort of ball-breaking bitch would do that to the man she vowed to love, honor, and care for till parted by death?"

"Can I talk to Bobby?"

The man laughs. "Are you *shitting* me? You didn't just say that."

"Please. I'd like to speak to Bobby."

He blinks like a jock in calculus class; as if trying to comprehend something beyond his mental capacity. "You'd like to speak to *Bobby*?"

"Yes."

"Pardon my sense of bewilderment, Megan. You see, the thing is...Bobby's been trying to talk to *you* for *eight* fucking *weeks*!"

Megan frowns. "Who *are* you?"

"Bobby calls me Mr. Witt. I see no reason you can't do the same."

"He hired you to steal the lottery money?"

"Absolutely not! Bobby didn't even know about the lottery money until earlier today. He has no idea we did this to you. And if he finds out, I can assure you he'll be very upset."

"Then I'm afraid I don't understand what this is—"

"You don't need to understand. But you *do* have to transfer the money."

Megan wipes the tears from her eyes; then asks the only question that truly matters. "After I do what you want...are you going to kill me?"

"Not today, Hon. Maybe tomorrow." He thinks a moment, then says, "I may not kill you at all. I *did* just say you could keep twenty grand, didn't I?"

Yes he did. But something in the way he said it tells Megan that being killed tomorrow is far more likely. Worse, she sees it in his eyes. Now that death seems imminent, her body and mind seem to be shutting down. She suddenly feels numb, and his words sound like someone's talking to her in a swimming pool, underwater. She feels her pulse shift from fast to out of control. It's thrumming in her ears. Megan needs something to cling to. If there's the slightest hope, she needs to hear it in his voice, or see it in his eyes. She stares into them, hoping to find...

Something.

Anything.

But doesn't.

Megan jumps straight to panic mode, and starts shivering violently. She can barely make her voice work. "Wh-what c-can I d-do t-t-to—?"

"I already told you. Transfer the money to your joint checking account so Bobby can access it."

"I-I mean, *after* th-that. Wh-what can I d-do to st-stay alive? I d-don't want to d-die."

"How do you feel about Bobby?"

"Wh-what do you m-mean?"

"Would you consider going back to him?"

The easy answer's yes. But something in his voice says he knows the truth. So she says, "I'd t-take him b-back to s-save m-my life."

"Well said. The words, if not the stutter. Is there any other reason you'd ever consider going back to him?"

"No."

"Because?"

"I-i d-don't l-love him."

"Did you ever?"

She thinks a moment. "P-probably n-not."

He nods, strokes her hair a moment. Then says, "You can't call the bank in this condition. They'll hear the stress in your voice."

"I-I'm s-s-sorry," Megan says.

"I'm sorry too. It means I have to turn you over to Bad Man again."

Chapter 28

"N-NO! P-please! I'll m-m-make the c-c-call!"

"I'd let you if I thought you could speak without trembling. But I can't afford to have your account manager hear you stuttering like this. She might think you're being coerced." He looks at her a moment, then gets an idea. "I'm willing to wait a few minutes for you to calm down, but we're running out of time." He checks his watch. "Bank closes in 45 minutes. Think you can get your shit together before then?"

She nods.

"Good, because you'll only get the one chance."

"After I d-do it, w-will you l-let me g-go?"

"How about we leave that decision to Bobby?"

What? Did he just say *Bobby* might decide her fate? It takes her mind several seconds to process his words. This is more than good news. It's perfect news!

Mr. Witt notices the difference. He says, "The relief on your face just elevated your looks two full points on the ten-scale!"

How could it not? Bobby would never sentence her to death. Not in a million years. Yes, she may have shafted him with the lottery money, but she knows Bobby loves her. Megan's aware Mr. Witt is speaking, but the pulse in her ears is drowning it out. Her thoughts are racing a mile a minute. Still, whatever he's saying is probably must-have information. She mentally screams, trying to force her brain to concentrate on his words. He's saying...

"Hard to believe, I know."

"S-sir?"

"You missed that? I said more than anything in the world Bobby wants you back. But unfortunately, you don't share his feelings."

She starts to say something, but he waves her off. "Yeah, I know what you're willing to do to stay alive, but that's no basis for a relationship."

"I d-*do* care wh-what happens t-to Bobby. I d-don't hate him."

His features soften slightly. "I'm not entirely lacking in compassion," he says. "Like I said, I'm willing to give you a chance to earn your freedom."

Things are looking up. She feels her body trying to restore itself. She's still shivering, but not as violently. She looks at him with hopeful eyes and waits for him to explain.

"You'd have to perform two challenges," Mr. Witt says. "The second one is you'll have to have sex with Bobby. That may not sound difficult, since it's something you've done a thousand times over the years, but the catch is he can't know it's you."

She looks at him with a combination of curiosity, frustration, and annoyance.

Mr. Witt says, "Bobby's expecting to be seduced by a movie star tonight." Noting her expression he chuckles and says, "No, of course it's not true, but that's the setup. Bobby thinks he's participating in an X-rated reality TV show."

Seeing her expression he smiles. "I know, right? But you of all people know how gullible Bobby is. He's a sweet guy, but...." He waves a hand in her general direction and says, "No matter. I think you'll agree perception is reality, and lucky for you, Bobby believes this scenario is real. And he *was* going to have sex tonight with a willing participant. It's just that she's not a movie star." He pauses. "I'm giving you more information than you require. I'll make it simple. I'll let you take the girl's place. If you want to live, I'll let you pretend you're the movie star who's trying to win money and a starring role in a TV show. Bobby's wrists will be cuffed to the bed and he'll be wearing a hood. You'll be as silent as you value your life, because a single whisper will guarantee your death. If at any time he suspects it's you–" He lifts the coiled rope over his head, tosses it to the floor and says, "– Bad Man will cut Bobby's throat and hang you on the spot. Understood?"

Megan nods.

"You can do whatever you want sexually, but he has to finish inside you. Afterward, we'll ask Bobby to rate the experience. If he gives you at least a nine, I'll spare your life."

The look she gives Mr. Witt makes it obvious she was expecting something better. Still, if anyone knows how to sexually please Bobby....

Mr. Witt says, "This isn't as random as it might seem. As I mentioned earlier, Bobby had sex last night. What I didn't tell you is he rated the young lady a nine, which is pretty damn good. A year ago it'd be a snap for you to match that, but these days you have no interest in him sexually. That being the case, you'll have to work awfully hard to earn an unbiased nine. But if you do, I'll let you live." He pauses a moment, then says, "I'll go you one better. If Bobby gives you a perfect ten, I'll give you an extra 80 grand. That might help Bobby get the most bang for his buck."

Megan wants to believe him, but didn't he just say perception was reality? She doesn't want to fall victim to his mind games like Bobby apparently has. She'd hate to humiliate herself by seducing Bobby if they're planning to kill her anyway. And what if she goes through the whole thing and Bobby gives her an eight? The idea of the rating gives his words the ring of truth, but she needs to hear him promise it. If he's lying, she'll be able to see it in his eyes.

Mr. Witt seems to sense her internal struggle. He says, "What's on your mind, little one?"

"You p-promise? To l-let me g-go?"

"I promise."

"Th-that's the s-second th-thing?"

"Yes. There are two challenges. As we've discussed, seducing Bobby is number two. Are you ready for number one?"

She nods.

"Stand, please, and remove your top."

With pleading eyes she asks him not to do this. Doesn't say a word, just lets her eyes do the begging. But it has no effect on him. He simply asks, "You want to live?"

She does. So without further hesitation, she stands, lifts her top over her head, and exposes two very average, very ordinary, breasts.

The expression on Mr. Witt's face is something between complete shock and udder disappointment. He stares at her tits like a kid who found socks in his last Christmas present. He says, "Not sure what I was expecting, but based solely on the degree of Bobby's devotion I thought at the very *least*...." He lets his voice trail off, then says, "No matter." He removes a lemon from his pocket, tears it in half. Rubs some citrus flesh on her nipples and sucks them till she gasps in pain 31 times. Nothing magical in the number of gasps, it's simply how many she happened to make before he achieved orgasm.

He takes two steps back to survey his work: Megan's nipples are distended, purple, and angry-looking. She's crying softly, but appears relieved the assault has ended.

"Say something," he says.

"Is this part over?"

He says, "Can you be more specific?"

"Did we complete the first challenge?"

"We did." He smiles broadly. "Are you aware you spoke the words perfectly just now?"

She is, but his smile galls her. Like she's supposed to be thankful she's suddenly able to make the phone call that will remove millions of dollars from her account? She wants to appear grateful, at least till he lets her go, but it's not going to be easy. This bastard caused her to be kidnapped, beaten, tortured physically and mentally. And now he's sucked five years of shape off her boobs. Megan looks at her nipples and wonders if he could've possibly done less damage with a cheese grater. She's not a violent person, but she'd kill Mr. Witt in a heartbeat. But since that doesn't appear to be a viable option she focuses on the two she has: die rich or live poor.

She takes a deep breath, then says, "I'm ready to make the call now."

"Excellent."

She does. Then they wait for the account manager to verify the transfer of funds. When that's done Megan clicks off her cell phone, turns to Mr. Witt and says, "What happens now?"

He takes her hand, kisses, it, and leaves the room. Megan stares at the closed door for five minutes. When it opens, Bad Man enters, walks over to her silently, puts his hand around her throat. She instinctively reaches both hands up in an effort to pry his grip loose, but as she attempts that, his other hand injects something cold into her hip.

Nothing happens for several seconds. Then a warm rush surges through her body. Megan feels Bad Man easing her to the floor. As she attempts to maintain her consciousness, she's vaguely aware some other people have entered the room. Men? Women?

Does it matter?

Not really.

When she opens her eyes she sees Bad Man standing over her, pressing a finger to his lips. What, she's supposed to be quiet? Fuck him. She opens her mouth to scream, but a familiar scent makes her stop. She closes her eyes, tries to clear the fog from her head. Next time she opens her eyes she realizes the floor she's lying on is cleaner than the one she passed out on. This one is tiled, not concrete. And again, her nose detects that familiar scent. She blinks her eyes, lolls her head to the side to get a better look, and realizes she's lying on the floor of Bobby's bathroom.

Bad Man signals her to be quiet, then whispers, "I've been instructed to let you take a shower. I asked if I could personally soap you down, but that request was denied. On the bright side, I *do* get to watch you."

He steps over her body and turns on the shower.

Chapter 29

MEGAN SQUEEZES HER eyes tightly, a combination of fury and helplessness. This bastard has beaten her repeatedly and without mercy. He tortured and terrorized her. Broke her spirit. The only consolation—if you could call it that—is she hasn't been stripped, fondled, or sexually assaulted. Much as she'd love to take a shower before seducing her husband, the idea of this man seeing her naked is more than she can bear.

"I'm okay," she whispers. "I'll forego the shower."

"You'll take a shower or suffer the consequences."

She starts to cry, and immediately regrets it when Bad Man punches the side of her head. "Shut the fuck up!" he hisses. He grabs her by the hair, pulls her to a standing position; then gives her neck a long, smelly lick with his tongue and whispers, "If you want, I can help you out of your clothes."

No, she *doesn't* want that. She steps past him and removes her clothes while keeping her back to him.

"Nice ass," he whispers as she enters the shower. Megan pulls the glass door shut, but he pulls it back open. She steps under the warm spray.

After a minute he whispers, "I've got a bar of soap for you, but you'll have to turn around to get it."

She reaches her hand behind her like a relay race sprinter waiting for the baton, but he says, "Nope. You'll have to turn around."

She turns halfway.

"Completely," he says.

She closes her eyes and does.

"Now reach out for it."

She does, and to her surprise, he hands her the soap without trying to grab or touch her.

"Thank you," she whispers.

"No, thank *you!*" he says.

A few minutes later he offers her some shampoo. Then a toothbrush and some toothpaste. Then some mouthwash.

And later, a towel.

The entire experience is creepy to the max, but she expected far worse. Having her tormenter see her naked nearly did her in, but now, draped in a towel, standing by the door that leads to Bobby's bedroom, she's trying to put the incident behind her.

Megan's hopeful.

Her situation seems to have improved dramatically. Yes, Bad Man leered at her in the grossest, most disgusting way. But he didn't touch her or make vulgar remarks, nor has he punched her since the moments before the shower. He also hasn't put the hood back on her head. Funny how quickly her perception of what constitutes bad treatment can change. In Megan's case she's been beaten, tortured, robbed, and somehow feels grateful for the chance to fuck her estranged husband well enough to be released.

She hears the bedroom door open, then a light tapping on the other side of the bathroom door. Bad Man opens the door, and Mr. Witt enters. He's carrying a pair of jeans, a sweatshirt, panties, socks, and running shoes. He whispers, "You can put these on when you're finished. I'm going to bring Bobby into the bedroom soon, so I'll ask you to remember the terms of our agreement. You're to say nothing, make no sounds, or attempt to signal him in any way. He can't know this is you. If he figures it out, our deal is off, and you won't leave the room alive. Understood?"

She nods.

He hands her a small sample-sized tube of perfume. "Dab this on," he says, then leaves the room, closes the door behind him. Megan turns to Bad Man and whispers, "Why all the beatings and torture?"

He shrugs. "I assume there's money involved."

"You know there is. But I agreed to pay before you hit me the very first time."

"What's your question?"

"Why did you beat me after I agreed to cooperate?"

"I like my job."

"What, beating up defenseless women?"

"Of course. Who wouldn't enjoy that?"

Megan frowns.

Bad Man says, "I'm just kidding. I worked you over because if I told them you volunteered to wire the money right away they might not feel I earned my fee."

"You beat me to validate your paycheck?"

"The first day, yes. But I *pretended* to beat you the third and fourth days. They don't know I didn't."

"Why are you telling *me?*"

"Because when you think back on this experience I hope you'll remember I could have treated you much worse."

His words hit her like week-old pastry: like useless, empty calories she doesn't want or need. He wants her to like him, but all she can think about is what he did to her. How he hurt her. How he hit her a few minutes ago, before she entered the shower, and how he made her keep the shower door open and how he made her turn around and...

"You filmed me in the shower," she says. "Is that why you made me turn around? So Mr. Witt could see me naked?"

He points to the camera on the wall. "It's not personal. I'm just following orders."

"So there's more to it than just taking my money."

"What do you mean?"

"I'm being punished."

"Of course you are."

"For what, exactly?"

"I'm just a grunt. They don't tell me shit, so I have no idea what you've done. But I know someone who does."

"Who?"

"You."

Megan bites her lip. He's right, of course, but which of the bad things she's done do they know about?

Chapter 30

MEGAN HEARS THE bedroom door open, hears Mr. Witt telling Bobby to remove his clothes and lie on his back on the bed. After a moment, he says, "I'll cuff you now." She hears the click of handcuffs. Then he reminds Bobby to say nothing, nor should he attempt to exchange any types of signals. She hears Bobby agree.

The way Megan's got it figured, Bobby found out about the lottery money and desperately tried to contact her. When she refused to take his calls or respond to his emails, he probably asked around and someone introduced him to Mr. Witt, who charged Bobby $10 million for kidnapping Megan and forcing her to transfer the balance of the lottery money into their joint account. Now Bobby can transfer it to his personal account. Mr. Witt probably took his cut Tuesday morning when she wired the money to his offshore account in the Bahamas.

The more she thinks about it the more she's convinced Bobby's fingerprints are all over this kidnapping. What did Mr. Witt say? Bobby sent his *regards*? Then asked if she'd consider going *back* to him? What sort of kidnapper would ask her that?

A kidnapper hired by Bobby.

Mr. Witt also said *Bobby* would make the decision as to whether or not she gets to live after transferring the money to their joint account.

And *how* would he decide?

By having her fuck him!

Megan's supposed to believe this is all Mr. Witt's idea? That if Bobby rates her sexual prowess a nine or better, he'll spare her life? Any idiot can see this is Bobby's way of forcing her to not only *fuck* him, but give him the best sex she possibly can. It's a complete turning of the tables, designed to put him in control. She didn't return his emails? Fine. Now she has to come to him, in his house. She didn't want him sexually? Fine. Now she has to seduce him and earn his highest rating.

It's disgusting.

Humiliating.

Infuriating.

Except for one thing: Bobby wouldn't do this. He wouldn't do any of these things. Wouldn't demand sex, wouldn't force himself on her, or any other woman.

Mr. Witt's right: he's gullible. He almost certainly believes he's on an X-rated TV reality show. Thinks he's being seduced by a movie starlet who's trying to earn some cash and a starring role.

What an idiot!

She shakes her head to force the negative thoughts from her mind. Because there's no way she can go into full seduction mode if she's thinking about her husband.

He repulses her.

But she's got to come through this, and do it with flying colors. So here's the plan: she'll give him the best sex she can, and if he rates her an eight or less, she'll reveal herself, and tell him that Mr. Witt threatened to kill her. If Bobby gives her a bad rating, what has she got to lose by screaming her name? It's a chance for life, and she's willing to take it.

She'd like to wring Bobby's neck for putting her in this situation, but she'll pony up, give him the best sex of his life, and allow him to "spare" her life. Whether or not Bobby knows the bulk of the lottery money is in their joint account, she knows he'll want to control it, if at all possible. He loves her, wants her back, and probably figures if he controls the money, she'll tear up the divorce papers and move back in with him.

And he's right.

About the divorce papers, anyway. She'll tear them up and initiate a new divorce proceeding, and the judge will award her half the money, and that's a helluva lot better than nothing. Maybe after that she'll devise a diabolical way to punish him for putting her in the situation that's about to happen right now.

Mr. Witt opens the door, and beckons her into the room. She hesitates long enough to stare at her husband lying on the bed. His hands are cuffed to the headboard, and there's a sheet covering him from the waist down. She needs to get her head right, but there's one thing she has to work out in her mind before she can focus on seducing Bobby. She needs to believe he never ordered her torture.

Is it possible Bobby hired Mr. Witt to steal the money?

Yes.

She doesn't think that's the case, but yes, it's possible.

If he did hire them, would Bobby have allowed them to rough her up a little so she'd believe she was being kidnapped? Possibly. Could he have sanctioned some mild beatings to help convince her to wire the first $10 million?

Doubtful.

Which brings us to torture.

Are there any circumstances under which Bobby would allow someone to literally set her feet on fire?

No.

Bobby may not be *her* Prince Charming, but he's a decent person. He's always been good to her, always treated her with respect. If Bobby hired Mr. Witt the only explanation for the torture is Bobby didn't know about it, and doesn't know about it now.

She looks at Mr. Witt, urging her toward the bed.

It makes sense he's the one who ordered the torture. He probably felt torturing her was the sure way to get his cut of the money—obviously $10 million—right off the bat.

That would explain why she hasn't been tortured since then. Mr. Witt already had *his* money, so anything else would've been gravy.

Mr. Witt gives her a warning look.

She nods. The good thing about putting her destiny in Bobby's hands is she's going to survive this ordeal. She knows what he likes in the bedroom, and how he likes it to happen. She'll disguise her technique, of course, but in the end he'll have no choice but to love what she does.

The trick is to focus on the money, and pretend he's someone else.

It helps that he's got a hood covering his head.

Not because he's ugly, but because if she squints her eyes just right his body sort of resembles Bradley Cooper's.

She takes a deep breath. Rule number one is survive. Later on she'll have lots of opportunities to make Bobby's life a living hell.

Megan approaches the bed, sits beside her husband, leans toward him, lifts the lower part of the hood to reveal his lips, and kisses him—not like a wife—but like a teenager in love. She turns to look at Mr. Witt and Bad Man and waits for them to leave the room, knowing full well they'll be watching the live feed from the video cameras on the wall surrounding the bed.

Nothing she can do about that, and anyway, they've already seen her naked, so how much worse can *this* be? As she removes the towel from her body she catches a glimpse of her boobs and decides to make it her life's mission to pay Mr. Witt back for everything he did to her this week.

She continues kissing Bobby like she means it, and allows her fingertips to caress his face.

He's responding.

She gives him time to bloom, then backs away and carefully removes the sheet. She looks at her husband's throbbing erection, and squints her eyes. Then thinks: *Oh, Bradley! Oh my God, I can't believe it's so big!*

And later: *You're gorgeous, Bradley! So, so gorgeous. I'm going to show you things no Hollywood starlet knows. I'm going to spoil you rotten, you bad little boy, and then I'm going to ruin you for every girl who follows. Whoever you're with, for the rest of your life, you're going to be silently screaming "Megan!"*

Megan gives him everything she's got, and finishes with a reverse cowgirl, something she never attempted previously.

When she's positive he's done she gets up, pads to the bathroom, gets a warm washcloth, brings it back, and cleans him up. Gives him one last, lingering kiss. Then kisses his penis, and covers him with the sheet.

Then she gets up and walks to the door as Mr. Witt enters.

"You lucky bastard!" he says, closing the door. Then adds, "I bet you're grinning like a zoo monkey under that hood. She's gone, feel free to speak. How was it?"

Bobby sighs.

Mr. Witt looks at Megan, puts his finger to his lips. Then says, "You can talk now, Bobby."

When he fails to do so, Mr. Witt says, "I need your rating right now, while it's fresh in your mind. So tell me, from one to ten, how good was she?"

Bobby clears his throat.

From the far side of the room, Megan leans forward, listening, knowing her fate's on the line.

Chapter 31

BOBBY STARTS TO say something, stops; thinks it through. First things first: he's certain this was the movie star, not Ivy.

Several things gave her away. First, the reverse cowgirl. As predicted, he could tell this girl was lighter, narrower in the hips, in better shape than Ivy. When you're on your back and a woman's rocking back and forth on top of you, 20 pounds makes a difference.

Second, surprisingly, she wasn't as tight as Ivy. He would've expected a young movie starlet's snatch to be as tight as a bull's ass in fly season, but Ivy had her beat.

And third, if he's being honest, this girl simply wasn't as good as Ivy. In Bobby's world, any sex rates a ten. But that doesn't mean all partners are equal. This morning he gave Ivy a 9. On that basis, this young lady's a 7. She did her best, but no question, Ivy did better. Maybe this one was nervous, or failed to find him attractive.

Fourth, she didn't seem to have as much experience as Ivy. She was tentative with her moves. And the reverse cowgirl at the end?

Painful.

The only reason he managed an orgasm is because, inexplicably, she stopped thrusting and just sort of wiggled for a minute, as if trying to decide what to do next.

Bottom line? The movie star hopeful gets a seven. A low 7.

"Bobby?" Mr. Witt says.

"Huh?"

"I need your answer. Your honest answer."

Megan knows her husband. She knows what the delay means. Bobby's evaluating the score in his mind. He doesn't want to hurt anyone's feelings, but he doesn't want to lie, either. A minute ago she would've bet money she earned a 10. But now?

Bobby says, "I'm going to rate her a 9."

Megan closes her eyes. *Thank God!* Her knees nearly buckle from relief.

Mr. Witt says, "Could you repeat that please?"

"Nine," Bobby says. "A solid 9."

Mr. Witt flashes Megan a genuine smile. He mouths the word *Congratulations*. To Bobby he says, "Sit tight, I'll be back in a few minutes to set you free." Then he quietly escorts Megan from the room.

Under the hood, Bobby smiles. It took him a few minutes to work out the strategy, but in the end, giving the hopeful movie star a solid 9 was brilliant. Had he given her the 7 she earned, Mr. Witt would tell Ivy she only has to beat a 7 tomorrow night. But if he tells her she has to beat a solid 9, Ivy will give him the best sex of his life. Of course, the joke will be on Ivy, because regardless of how well she does tomorrow night, he plans to give her a 6. The movie star will get the job and the cash bonus, and Ivy will be properly punished for leaving him handcuffed with a key shoved up his ass.

Mr. Witt and Bad Man walk Megan through the house, into the garage. Then Mr. Witt says, "I couldn't help but notice you were limping just now."

Megan doesn't really give a shit what this tit-sucking bastard notices, as long as he sets her free. But since he mentioned her limp....

She looks at Bad Man, then at Mr. Witt. "Perhaps it's because he set my *feet* on fire?"

Mr. Witt chuckles. "Probably. But don't worry, you'll heal quickly. I'm certain of that."

"Does that mean you're going to keep your promise?"

"Regarding the seduction, I'm impressed. That couldn't have been easy for you, since Bobby seems to repulse you, and yet you came through with flying colors. Despite what you might think, I'm very happy for you."

"Does that mean you're going to keep your promise?"

"Short answer? Yes. Longer answer? There's a caveat."

Megan frowns.

Mr. Witt says, "Don't feel betrayed. It's not so bad. The caveat is you have to keep your mouth shut about everything that's happened. Can you do that?"

"Yes."

He cocks his head. "Everything, Megan."

"I understand."

He says, "Human nature dictates you'll eventually tell someone. The day I hear about it, you die. Fair enough?"

She nods. "I can really go?"

"Yes."

"Right now?"

"If you like. You can walk out now, or call someone to pick you up. I'd drive you myself, except that I promised Bobby I'd set him free. I assume you'd rather be gone by then?"

"Yes. I'll go now, and call someone to meet me a couple of blocks from here."

"In that case you'll need your phone."

He looks at Bad Man.

Bad Man reaches in his pocket, pulls out Megan's phone. But as he hands it to her his head explodes.

Chapter 32

MEGAN'S FACE AND torso is covered in blood, bone, and brain bits. She screams, and keeps screaming. From the garage door landing behind them, Kennon shrieks.

As he's diving to the floor, Mr. Witt thinks, *Kennon's here?*

He hits and rolls, locates the shooter: a young blonde, and her weapon, a high-tech handgun equipped with a silencer. He reaches for the cyanide cylinder, but as his hand clears his pocket, she fires a bullet through his palm, and the cylinder skitters across the floor.

Mr. Witt cries out in pain. That, plus Kennon's gasping, and Megan's howling, causes the blonde to yell, "Shut the fuck up!"

Kennon and Mr. Witt go silent immediately.

Megan, trying for empathy, points at Bad Man's body. The problem for her, the corpse never hit the ground. When he fell against the car, the rear-view mirror snagged his armpit. It's holding him upright, and the blood spurting from his wound causes his half-head to loll back and forth like a *Walking Dead* cast member trying to watch a tennis match.

The blonde motions Kennon to enter the garage. Spying the purse slung over her shoulder, Mr. Witt remembers the ice pick and wonders if Kennon might consider elevating her game from property damage to murder.

The blonde, speaking to Kennon, says, "I'm sorry you had to see this. Even sorrier you'll have to help put the body in Bobby's trunk. But it's going to take all three of you to manage it." Megan says, "B-but...h-he's..."

"Hung up on the mirror? No problem." The blonde shoots Bad Man's shoulder once, twice, a third time. Then says, "Wait for it..."

It takes a couple of seconds, but the weight of Bad Man's body gradually becomes too much for the shattered shoulder to support. As it separates, it makes a strange sucking sound, like when you're a kid, and your shoe gets stuck in mud and you have to pull it out. After Bad Man's shoulder makes that sound, his arm severs completely from his body, and remains hooked on the mirror.

But the body slides to the floor.

Megan suppresses a scream, apparently deciding this view is less terrifying than the prior one. She recovers enough to say, "I-I'd like to g-go now."

The blonde stares at her with amusement.

Megan explains, "Mr. Witt s-said I could g-go f-free if I d-did the th-things he asked. I d-did them, and n-now I'd like to l-leave."

The blonde says, "That's not going to happen, Megan."

Mr. Witt says, "Megan's probably wondering who she has to fuck *this* time to go free."

"*Sh-shut up, a-asshole!*" Megan shouts. "I h-hope you r-rot in hell!" She looks at the blonde and says, "Why c-can't you l-let me go? I won't t-tell anyone wh-what happened h-here."

The blonde says, "Sorry Megan, but you're like rock and roll."

"W-What d-do you m-mean?"

"You're here to stay."

Mr. Witt, clearly in pain, attempts a smile. "I feel like I'm judging a beauty pageant, and the top three contestants are a blonde, a brunette, and a redhead!" He makes his smile warmer, and more sincere. Asks the blonde, "Would you consider calling me Andrew?"

"You think it'll help us bond?"

"Stranger things have happened."

"Not to me."

"Give us a chance. I might grow on you. What's your name, dear?"

"Callie."

He gives her a curious look. "Did...did you say...*Callie*? My *niece's* name is Callie."

"No it isn't, Andrew. And you just proved what a shameless, lying, sack of shit you are."

Mr. Witt pauses, makes a brave attempt to chuckle; gives up. Then says, "Bravo. I took it too far and you called me on it. Nice to meet you, Callie. He glances at the headless fence post that used to be Bad Man. "Can I ask what you do for a living?"

"I kill people."

"Oh, happy day. On the bright side, I'll probably bleed to death before you can kill me."

"Wanna bet?"

"No. And suddenly the thought of losing millions of dollars seems trivial."

"Glad you feel that way. I didn't actually come here for the money, though I'll *take* it, since I'm already here."

"Why *did* you come, Miss—"

"Carpenter," Callie says. "I came for Megan. Now I find myself in a small enclosure, surrounded by evil."

"Wh-what are you g-going to d-do? with m-me?" Megan says.

"What a perfectly-timed question! I'm so glad you asked."

Chapter 33

Ten Minutes Later...

"BOBBY, IT'S ME, Kennon."

"*Kennon?* Are you the one who just...uh..."

"No."

"Then...why are you *here?*"

She removes his hood and he notices her swollen eyes and tears. "What's wrong?"

"Everything."

"Where's Mr. Witt?"

"He made a recording."

She puts her phone on speaker and presses the play button.

Bobby hears Mr. Witt say,

> "Bobby? I kept my promise. If you'll remember, I
> promised to find a way to reunite you and Megan,

and I did. The young lady you had sex with a few minutes ago? That was Megan. Your wife."

"What?"
He looks at Kennon.
She nods.
Mr. Witt's voice continues:

"I made your dream come true. Megan's in your home, and she'll remain with you as long as you wish."

Bobby calls her name, notices fresh tears in Kennon's eyes.
"Let me *go*, Kennon!"
Mr. Witt's message ends with:

"Goodbye, Bobby. Enjoy the Bahamas."

Bobby looks at Kennon. "Where's my wife?"
Kennon takes a deep breath. "We haven't got much time. I'll remove the cuffs, but you need to hear me out first. Will you do that? Please?"
Bobby nods.
"It's true the woman you had sex with was your wife, Megan."
"That *can't* be true. I would have known."
"It was Megan, Bobby. I swear on my life. Also, sadly, there's video proof."
He looks around. "Where is she?"

"In the garage."

"Why?"

"It's—I don't want to say."

"Fine. I'll let *her* tell me."

"Bobby? Listen to me. Megan didn't win the lottery. She stole the winning ticket from her sister."

"I already figured that out. So what? Faith is obviously dead, or she would have cashed the ticket herself. She and Megan were close. She'd want Megan to have the money."

"When Megan cashed the ticket, some bad people decided to rob her."

"Which bad people?"

Kennon sighs. "Me."

Bobby blinks. "*What?*"

"I'm the one who interviewed you in Bowling Green for the reality show. My voice was electronically distorted. Mr. Witt has been working for me."

"That's not possible. He asked me all kinds of questions about you. He'd never seen you before, never met you, I'm sure of it."

"I never revealed myself to him. He never knew I had anything to do with it."

"I have no idea what you're talking about, nor do I care. I just want to talk to Megan. Seriously, Kennon. Get me out of these cuffs. I need to see her."

"Bobby, listen to me. You're running out of time. You're being framed for murder."

He nods. "I know. Nat Bailey. But it's not a frame up. I-I've been out of my head the last few days. I know you tried to help me with the flat tire and all, but—"

Kennon sighs. "Okay. I'll set you free now."

She does.

Bobby says, "Garage?"

She nods.

He jumps off the bed, starts for the door, realizes he's naked, turns to see if Kennon saw him. If she did, she's not reacting. She's staring straight ahead, vacantly. Bobby finds his pants, pulls them on, starts shouting Megan's name as he runs through the house toward the garage. When he opens the door, turns on the lights, he sees a pool of blood. Sees more blood on the passenger side of his car. Sees a trail of blood leading to the trunk of his car.

"*Megan!*" he shouts.

He runs to the car, tries to open the trunk.

It's locked.

He pounds his fists on the trunk, calls her name again and again, then stops to listen.

Hears nothing.

From the landing, Kennon says, "She's not in the trunk, Bobby."

"She is. Look at the blood. Please. Where are the car keys?"

Kennon tosses him a key. Bobby looks at it, then looks at Kennon.

She points to the freezer on the far wall.

It takes Bobby a second to realize the key in his hand works the freezer lock, but less than five more seconds to cross the floor and open the freezer. He throws the lid up and sees, to his horror, his dead wife.

He screams, starts trying to pull her out.

"*Help me!*" he shouts.

Kennon goes to his side, helps him pull the body out. Bobby lays Megan out on the floor, starts giving her CPR.

Kennon says, "She's dead, Bobby."

"No. She's barely even cold."

"Look at her face. She's been beaten half to death."

"Why?"

"That wasn't my doing. I trusted the wrong person. Then a killer entered the home tonight and gave Megan a lethal injection. In the back of her neck."

"That's ridiculous. Mr. Witt paid you to say that," Bobby says, but turns his wife onto her stomach, sees the dot where the needle broke the skin. "Help me, Kennon. Please! Call an ambulance!"

"She's dead, Bobby. And you need to get out of here."

"Are you *crazy?* Call 911! *Now*, Kennon!"

"*Listen to me!*" Kennon says. "She's dead. And you've got to get out of here!"

Bobby jumps to his feet. "If *you* won't call them, I will."

"You don't understand. I was here when Callie Carpenter killed her. She's dead, Bobby."

"No. We need to save her."

"She's past saving."

"No. We need to—"

Kennon rolls Megan onto her back, lifts one of her arms, lets it fall. "She's dead. I saw the whole thing. It wasn't my doing, or even Mr. Witt's. He set her free. But Callie Carpenter—"

"Who?"

"The contract killer. We knew nothing about her. Apparently Megan caused someone's death several months ago, someone Callie knew. She came here to kill Megan tonight, and did."

"No."

"You saw the blood? That was the guy who beat Megan up. Miss Carpenter killed him, too. Shot him in the head. He's the one who kidnapped Megan, and forced her to wire the money. But that wasn't part of my plan. The kidnapping was, but not the beating. Mr. Witt hired this guy and gave him that directive without my knowledge. I didn't know about it until this afternoon."

Bobby falls onto Megan's body and starts crying.

Kennon says, "She didn't love you, Bobby. Maybe a long time ago she did, but certainly not lately. She wouldn't even answer your emails. The only reason she came here tonight was to save her life. After the sex, when Mr. Witt told her she could leave or stay here with you, she wanted to leave. But then Miss Carpenter showed up."

When it finally dawns on Bobby his wife is dead, he closes his eyes for several minutes, sits beside her, and rocks back and forth. Kennon sits too, and drapes her arm over Bobby's shoulders. After a while he turns to her and says, "What was Mr. Witt talking about when he said to have fun in the Bahamas?"

"He meant with me."

Bobby lowers himself onto Megan's body for another minute, then raises up. "What did you just say?"

Chapter 34

"MY PLAN WAS simple," Kennon says, "but Mr. Witt went rogue. I hired him to kidnap Megan, hold her till she wired $10 million to an account in the Bahamas. Mr. Witt and I were going to split the money. But he hired a goon to kidnap her and beat her up. Then he made her wire the money to your joint account. I didn't know anything about that, but apparently he was planning to kill Megan and frame you for her murder. That's why he made her have sex with you tonight. She's dead, your sperm's inside her, and tens of millions of dollars were wired to your joint account. You could have either paid him off or gone to prison for the rest of your life."

"You said he told Megan she could go."

"Yes. But I'm pretty sure his goon was planning to kill her before she left the house."

"Is the money still in our joint checking account?

"No. it's disappeared, thanks to whatever Callie Carpenter has done. But none of that matters now, because when Megan's body is found, and the wire transactions traced, the feds are going to be all over you for the murder."

"You saw her get killed. You can be my witness."

"Sorry, but I want to live."

"You'd let me go to prison for something I didn't do?"

"Short of putting my life on the line? No. That's why I'm trying to get us out of the country."

"Right. To the Bahamas. What does that even *mean?*"

"It means I talked Callie Carpenter into sparing our lives. Yours and mine."

Bobby looks at his wife's body, traces his index and middle fingers gently across her face. He leans over her, kisses her lips. Looks up at Kennon and says, "This is all *your* fault!"

"The kidnapping and robbery were my fault. Not the beating or killing. Try to remember, Callie was going to kill Megan anyway. That's why she came to town. If I'd never met you or Megan, it wouldn't matter, Megan would still be dead."

Kennon hands Bobby his car keys. "The goon who tortured Megan is in your trunk. I asked Callie to kill him for what he did to her, and she was happy to oblige."

"Why?"

"She likes me."

Bobby gets up, goes to the trunk, opens it, sees Bad Man's body and severed arm, and nearly throws up. He slams the trunk shut and says, "Where's Mr. Witt?"

Kennon leads him back into the house, opens the hall closet door.

Bobby sees Mr. Witt on the floor, dead.

"He can't be dead. He just left the bedroom 15 minutes ago."

"Callie made him record the message on my phone, then killed him."

"You were there when he died?"

"No. But she explained what was going to happen, and told me to wait for at least two minutes before removing your hand cuffs."

"Whatever that bitch told you was a lie. Megan would never take someone's life."

Kennon says, "I don't know how to answer that. If she wasn't guilty, Callie Carpenter wouldn't have killed her."

"Who is she supposed to have killed?"

"Donovan Creed's daughter."

"Who's he?"

"A friend of Callie's."

"Creed's daughter was in the hospital in Louisville, Kentucky a couple months ago. Megan was called there to render an opinion on her condition. Callie says Ryan Decker, the terrorist, paid Megan to rub something on Kimberly Creed's skin. She did, and Kimberly's condition deteriorated quickly. Hours later, Megan pronounced her brain dead."

"That's bullshit."

"Not according to Megan."

"What do you mean?"

"She confessed that Decker got to her before she went in to examine Creed's daughter. He told her he had people watching her sister, her parents, and you. Said she could rub the compound on Kimberly's skin or she and the rest of you would die. Or, he'd give her $50,000 cash and allow you all to live. She said you had lost your job and money was tight and when she took the money she made up a story about cashing in her accrued vacation and sick days so no one would get suspicious."

"You heard her say all this?"

Kennon nods. "She claims she had no choice, and I believe her."

Bobby thinks about it a minute, then says, "So I'm supposed to what, run away with you to the Bahamas?"

"If you'll have me."

"What about your boyfriend?"

"There's no boyfriend."

"Another lie?"

She nods, then reaches into her handbag, removes a packet of cash, two plane tickets, and a folded piece of paper.

Bobby notes the tickets are in his name and hers. "Flight leaves in three hours?"

"Two-and-a-half."

"Where did the cash come from?"

"It's my life's savings."

"Why give it to me?"

"I wanted you to know I'm sincere. If we're going together, I'll share it with you. If you choose not to take me with you, it's yours."

"Why?"

"It could take a couple of days to access the money. In the meantime, you'll need cash for hotels, food, whatever."

He opens the folded piece of paper. "What's this?"

"The offshore bank account number, and the name and address of a guy who can get you a fake ID. Because you're not going to want to stay in the Bahamas long."

"Why give *me* the account number?"

"You've been through a lot. You deserve to get something out of it. And like I said, I'm hoping we can do this together."

"We'd go as a couple? You'd consider living together?"

"No. But I'm agreeable to friendship, and possibly dating."

"And the money?"

"There's $10 million in the account. I'm hopeful you'd split it with me."

"And if I don't?"

She shrugs. "I'll deal with it."

He pauses a moment, then says, "Tell me about the reality TV show."

"The whole thing was a hoax."

"What about the money Mr. Witt had the producers send? It was supposed to be here tomorrow."

"There's no reality show, Bobby. No producers. No actors. No check in the mail."

"What was the purpose? Why go to all that trouble?"

"Mr. Witt's idea. He wanted to distract you from contacting Megan, or contacting the police if you found out she was missing. He also hoped to keep you from cooperating with the police if they learned she was missing."

"He talked me into killing Nat Bailey."

"I gathered that, from the look on your face when the detectives showed up. But I had nothing to do with any of that. I *do* think the detectives would have taken you to jail if I hadn't slashed your tire."

He looks at Megan, then back at Kennon. "I agree. And part of me wants to believe everything you're saying."

"I didn't have to tell you all this, and didn't have to give you all my savings. But if we're going to have any chance at all as a couple, or even as friends, I wanted you to know everything I did."

"You never apologized."

"Not true, Bobby. I've been apologizing all this time. I told you everything. I gave you the account number, which means you're in complete control of all the money I could have kept for myself. I talked Miss Carpenter into sparing your life, and talked her into killing the two men who were responsible for beating and torturing Megan. I protected you from the detectives, who are certain to come here tonight or tomorrow morning at the latest. I've packed your bags, and mine, and bought you a ticket with my own money. I've also given you enough cash to get started. And yes, Bobby, I'm terribly, horribly sorry for my part in all this. But Megan never wanted you, and there's plenty of video and recorded evidence to prove that."

"So you say."

She pulls her cell phone from her purse, searches for an audio file, activates the speaker, presses a button. Bobby hears a conversation between Mr. Witt and Megan:

"How do you feel about Bobby?"
"Wh-what do you m-mean?"
"Would you consider going back to him?"
"I'd t-take him b-back to s-save m-my life."
"Well said. The words, if not the stutter. Is there any other reason you'd ever consider going back to him?"
"No."
"Because?"
"I don't love him."
"Did you ever?"
"Probably not."

Bobby looks at Kennon a moment, as if he just lost everything he wanted in life. "It's her voice," he says.

"She didn't love you, Bobby."

"She cheated on me with that Nat Bailey guy."

"She also hired an attorney to cheat you out of the lottery money."

Bobby nods. "I've been a fool."

"You were in love. I think you're noble."

He looks at her. "You're the prettiest woman I've ever seen—"

"Thank you."

"—But there's no way in hell I could ever trust you. I'd never be able to look at you without believing you had something to do with killing my wife."

"We might be able to overcome that, in time."

"Kiss me."

"What?"

"Kiss me."

"On the cheek?"

"No. A real kiss."

She shakes her head. "We're not at that point yet."

"That's what I thought."

He tears up her ticket, pinches half the money from the envelope, hands it to her. "I'm not going to share the ten million with you."

Kennon frowns. "Because I wouldn't kiss you?"

"Because you never will. And because I could never trust you. And because you asked a woman to kill two men."

"I did that for *you!*"

"Yes. But you also carry an ice pick in your purse. You're an incredibly dangerous person, and I cringe to think what might happen to me if I ever disappointed you or pissed you off."

"I get that, though I'm sorry you feel that way."

"So what are you going to do, call the detectives and have me arrested before my plane takes off?"

"No. You're free to go. Your bag's in the kitchen. While you're getting ready, I'll clean the blood off your car."

"I'm supposed to drive to the airport with a body in my trunk?"

"I would, if I were you. I doubt anyone will find the body for at least a week. If you left it here, they'd find it straight away."

"You'd actually clean the blood off my car?"

She nods. "Technically, I'm still on the clock."

"I can't figure you out."

"Take me with you, Bobby. I promise you won't regret it. I'm a very caring, loyal friend."

"Sorry."

Bobby punches a number on his cell phone. When Kaylee answers, he says, "Do you still want to date me?"

"Yes, of course!"

"How about tonight?"

"When?"

"Right now."

"How should I dress?"

"Like you're going to the Bahamas."

She giggles. "Am I?"

"You are."

"Wait. For *real?*"

"I swear!"

When he hangs up, Kennon says, "Seriously, Bobby?"

He winks. "Looks aren't everything, Kennon."

"Whatever. Have a nice life, Bobby."

"You too."

Chapter 35

AFTER CALLIE AND Kennon drag Mr. Witt's body to the garage and lay it out beside Megan's, Callie says, "Let me get this straight. Bobby's on his way to the airport? And he's taking a different girl to the Bahamas?"

Kennon nods.

"How does that make you feel?"

"Like he's not worthy of my friendship."

"You went to all this trouble for nothing."

"I'll be fine. He's the big loser, not me."

"How do you figure?"

"I was basically honest with him. I told him nearly everything, offered him my friendship, half my savings, and $5 million in cash."

"But he said no."

"He did. And it's his loss."

"You're talking about your friendship?"

"Yes."

"Still, he gains $10 million instead of five."

"Not really. I was testing him."

"What do you mean?"

"Bobby's been making choices ever since Bowling Green. I lied to him about the reality show. That was my idea, not Mr. Witt's. I've been testing him all along, testing the type of person he was, evaluating the choices he made. I'm not stupid, Callie. I offered him $5 million, but I gave him a phony bank account number. Had he been willing to share the money, and accept my friendship, I would have given him half."

Callie laughs. "You get the full $10 million?"

"I do."

"Then why aren't you smiling?"

"I'd rather have half the money and a good friend."

"Five million buys lots of friends, Kennon."

"I disagree."

Callie studies Kennon's face. "I've never met anyone like you. I'd be proud to be your friend."

Kennon studies Callie's face. "Does that mean you'd consider giving me half the money you stole from Bobby's joint checking account?"

"Honestly? Sure, why not? Except that I'm putting the entire sum into a scholarship fund in Kimberly Creed's name. I think Donovan would like that."

"I was willing to part with $5 million for Bobby's friendship. I'm sure Kimberly's scholarship fund could survive on less than what you've taken."

"How much less?"

"Five million?"

"How about one million?"

"I'll take it."

Callie looks into Kennon's eyes. "I'll give you a million dollars for your friendship...and a kiss."

"On the cheek?"

"No. A real kiss."

"Sorry. That wouldn't be honest."

Callie smiles. "I like you. No cash, but you can consider me a friend whether you want me or not. Type in my phone number as I call it out."

Kennon does. Then Callie says, "How long before the detectives show up?"

Kennon glances at her watch. "Ten minutes, give or take. Why?"

"I need to get these bodies in my trunk. You think they'd do that for me?"

"If you pay them."

Callie laughs. "I can't believe Mr. Witt couldn't tell they were fake detectives."

"They're pretty convincing. They were my backup plan, in case Mr. Witt and his gangster decided to shaft me."

"Can you fight?"

"Fight? What do you mean?"

"Kickboxing? Martial arts?"

"No."

"Want to learn?"

"Not really. Why?"

"I'd like to hire you."

Kennon laughs. "To *kill* people?"

"It's a good living. If you're good at it."

Kennon says, "I'm better at planning."

"But you *have* killed."

"When I've had to."

Callie chuckles. "I'd give anything to see the look on Bobby's face when he gets to the Bahamas and learns you gave him a phony account number!"

"Maybe he and Kaylee will find a way to build a new life together. I hope so."

"How much did you give Bobby for the trip?"

"Four thousand."

"Is that really the total of your life's savings?"

Kennon smiles.

Callie shakes her head. "I'm impressed. I like you."

"I like you, too, Callie....I think." Kennon looks at the bodies. "How long before they wake up?"

"Couple of hours."

"How'd you keep Megan from suffocating in the freezer?"

"Pulled the plug and kept the lid open till the last possible minute. Figured she had about five minutes of oxygen. You got there in two. She'll be fine."

"Where are you taking them?"

"It's better you don't know."

Chapter 36

Fifteen Minutes Earlier...

MEGAN'S KNEES GIVE way. She falls to the floor and starts twitching. She hasn't fainted; it's more like her body shut down to develop a coping mechanism. She eventually turns her head upward toward Callie's face.

"You believe I'll do it?" Callie says.

How could she not? The way Callie said it, the way her eyes went from flat to vacant when she shot Mr. Witt's hand, the fact she shot a man's head off moments ago—is pretty convincing. But if Megan has to die, she'd like to know the reason. She opens her mouth to ask, but the words won't come.

Callie says, "I know everything, Megan. You're what we call Dead Bitch Walking."

Mr. Witt says, "What did she do?"

"She murdered a hospital patient named Kimberly Creed."

Megan's eyes turn to fire. It's hard to sound indignant while stuttering, but she does her best. "I n-n-never k-killed anyone in m-my *life!*"

Callie smiles. "You should think twice before lying to me."

"I'm n-not—"

Callie closes the distance between them in the blink of an eye. Before Megan can even turn her head, Callie's got her by the neck, forcing her mouth open wide enough to accommodate the gun.

"Confess now," Callie says, "or die. You must know I'm serious."

She removes the gun and Megan stammers out her confession. According to her, she had no choice but to kill Kimberly.

"That wasn't so hard, was it?" Callie says. Then adds, "By the way, the resemblance is uncanny."

The words hit Megan hard.

"Resemblance?" Mr. Witt says.

Callie says, "She's battered and bruised, and covered with blood. But the resemblance is unmistakable. Truly remarkable."

Mr. Witt says, "What resemblance?"

"You didn't know? Megan's an identical twin."

Mr. Witt stares at her. "Identical to whom?"

"Her sister. Faith Stallone."

"Wait. The one who went missing? Are you saying Megan killed her *sister?*"

"No. But she stole Faith's winning lottery ticket."

"I don't understand."

Megan says, "She'd b-been m-missing for w-weeks. It s-seemed s-stupid to let the t-ticket go to w-waste."

Mr. Witt looks at Callie. "Are you going to kill us all?"

"I might spare one of you. Any suggestions which one?"

"Me."

"Why?"

"I'm the only one who's married. My wife is very dependent on me."

"You love her?" Callie says.

"More than anything."

"How long have you been married?"

"Eight years."

"Any rough patches?"

He shrugs. "Same as any marriage, I suppose."

"Women, right?" Callie says.

He chuckles. "Any chance we can have a doctor look at my hand?"

"No. But I'll look at it after Bobby leaves."

"Bobby? Where's he going?"

Callie looks at Kennon. "The Bahamas?"

Kennon nods.

Mr. Witt's face morphs. "Are you and Kennon affiliated in some way?"

"No."

"Then how does she know about the Bahamas?"

Callie sighs. "You're aware we've been standing in Bobby's garage all this time with a dead body, right?"

Mr. Witt says, "You used a silencer."

"True, but you and Megan did more shrieking than a Megadeth tribute band. What do you suppose the neighbors think about that?"

"No one's called or come by."

"Weird, don't you think?"

Mr. Witt shrugs.

Megan says, "Wh-what happens t-to me?"

"I'm afraid you're on borrowed time."

"*W-why*? Wh-what have I *d-done*?"

"Apart from your annoying stutter? You made a bad career choice. Should have tried a different medical specialty."

Mr. Witt says, "Can I ask what her specialty is?"

Callie frowns. "You don't *know*? What type of thief *are* you?"

"I didn't think her job was relevant to kidnapping her and forcing a money transfer."

"*Everything's* relevant, Andrew. You'd do well to remember that. Megan's a brain death specialist for the Academy of Neurology."

"Impressive. Still, I'm not sure why that's relevant to—"

"It's relevant to my being here, which cost you $5 million."

"Well...wait. How did you know my fee was—"

"Andrew?"

He looks at her.

"I'm not going to wrap things up for you like some TV detective in the final segment. I've got too much to do, and anyway, Bobby's yelling for you to set him free."

He cocks his head. "He is?"

"You can't *hear* him?"

"I can," Kennon says.

"Good girl. Andrew? You know what I'd like?"

He shakes his head.

"I'd like to either kill you, or meet your wife, Betty. Your choice."

"My...uh...Betty?"

Callie lifts the gun toward his face for the second time.

Mr. Witt says, "Consider it done!"

"Good man. So it's set. Later tonight, we'll go to the cottage."

His face blanches. "The cottage?"

"Yes. So I can meet Betty."

"Actually, I'm afraid Betty's not at her best around strangers."

"I'm willing to bet she'll be happy to see *me*, under the circumstances."

Callie points at the freezer in the corner. "Is it locked?"

Kennon nods.

"You have the key?"

"We keep it above the door."

Callie leads the trio back in the house, tells Mr. Witt to record a message to Bobby on Kennon's phone. Tells him what to say. When that's done, she motions him to enter the hall closet. As he does, she stabs the back of his neck with a syringe and closes the door before he hits the floor.

"Kennon?" she says. "I noticed Bobby fixed his tire."

"Yes."

"And did you manage to stay busy while he did that?"

She nods.

Callie says, "Let's go back to the garage." She leads the girls back to the garage and motions them toward the freezer, tells Kennon to open it. Kennon reaches above the door jamb for the key, finds it, unlocks the freezer, then lifts the lid. Callie says, "Megan? Did Mr. Witt personally take part in beating you?"

She looks apprehensively at the freezer, then at Callie. "N-no. B-but he..."

"Yeah?"

"Abused me."

She lifts her shirt.

Callie says, "Are those bite-marks?"

Megan nods.

"Ouch, that's got to hurt. What a bastard! Don't worry, I'll see he's properly punished for that." She nods at the freezer and says, "Okay then, climb in, sit down, and put your head between your knees."

"*What?*"

"Now, please."

Megan shrieks, and goes into full freak mode to the point Callie has to backhand her to calm her down. "Would you rather I blow your head off?"

No she wouldn't. But she'd like to beg for her life, and does so.

"Sorry," Callie says. "But you earned this."

Megan turns to Kennon. "*Please!*" she says. "*Do something.*"

Kennon looks at Callie.

Callie says, "You want to do something? Fine. You can help her get in the freezer."

Megan falls to the floor and starts sobbing.

Callie grits her teeth. "Don't let anyone tell you this shit is easy," she says.

She moves closer, takes a knee, waits for the thrashing girl to expose her chin. When she does, Callie delivers a knockout blow to Megan's jaw. Then tells Kennon to help lift her into the freezer. When that's done, Callie removes a second syringe from her bag, empties it in Megan's neck. Then gets the key from Kennon and says, "I'll put it back above the door when I'm done. You still want to help Bobby?"

Kennon nods.

"You're packed?"

"Yes."

"And the tickets?"

"I printed them while he changed the tire."

"Good. Need cash for the trip?"

"No, but thank you."

Kennon looks at the freezer a long moment. When she turns back to Callie there are tears streaming down her face.

"That's adorable!" Callie says. "You didn't even know her, but you're crying for her. She doesn't deserve it. Believe me."

Kennon pauses a moment, then says, "Can I tell Bobby the truth?"

"About?"

"My part in all this?"

"I wouldn't. Why would you even consider doing that?"

"I think he deserves to know. Especially if we're going to start a relationship."

Callie sighs, shakes her head. "Suit yourself."

"You think he'll leave without me?"

"If you tell him the truth, yeah. I'm certain of it."

They look at each other a moment, Callie getting the better of it. "If he leaves without you," she says, "I'd love the chance to get to know you better."

Kennon says, "I know. But...I can't do that. I'm sorry."

Callie smiles. "I know you can't." She sighs again. "What a waste."

Kennon says, "I better go free Bobby."

Callie says, "I'll be out of sight, but the house is wired."

"I know."

"I'm just reminding you so you won't try anything stupid. It would ruin my day to kill you, and that's the truth. Uh...by the way, the joint checking account? Thanks for cooperating."

Kennon says, "I didn't have much choice, did I?"

"No, but you could have made it more difficult."

"Well...you're welcome."

Epilogue

"WHERE WILL YOU go?" Callie says.

"Vegas, I think. Then the Bahamas."

"I have a condo in Vegas."

Kennon says, "I'm straight, Callie."

"Relax. The condo's going to be empty for a year. I'm just saying...."

"Are you taking an extended vacation?"

"I'm planning to buy a cottage in the woods and live there a while."

"That sounds relaxing."

"I'd love for you to use my condo while you're in Vegas."

"Well...perhaps for a month. Thank you. That's very thoughtful."

"Do you have family there?"

"I have a connection."

"Anyone I know?"

"I doubt it. She's young, ambitious, as we tend to be."

"We?"

"There's a group of us."

"Like a club?"

She purses her lips. "In a way."

"Well, if the others are anything like you, I'd like to apply for membership."

"Hug me."

"Seriously?"

Kennon nods.

They hug a moment, then Kennon backs away.

Callie says, "What was that about?"

"I was positive you weren't an intuitive, but I thought I should check, just in case."

"Not sure what you're talking about, but if you want a *real* hug, I'd like another shot."

Kennon smiles. "There are lots of descendants of Jack Hawley, the pirate, but a very few of us, the intuitive ones, can recognize each other with a touch, or hug. In some cases we can tell from miles away."

"That explains it."

"What?"

"Since meeting you earlier today I couldn't figure out how someone so gorgeous and sweet could walk around with an ice pick in her purse, kidnap a woman, and steal her money. You also admitted to killing people when you had to."

"And what conclusion have you drawn?"

"You're a pirate, and the ice pick is your sword. Looting and kidnapping is what pirates do. It's in your blood!" She pauses, then says, "Your club is comprised of pirates."

"Harsh label."

"You think? Try telling your new girlfriend's parents you're an assassin!"

Kennon laughs.

Callie says, "I believe my friend, Donovan Creed, may have met a young lady in Florida who was descended from Jack Hawley. She had some sort of healing gift."

"Libby Vail?"

"I'm not sure. Could be."

"Libby's one of us."

"Is she in Vegas?"

"No. She's taking a different path."

"Toward what?"

"We're building our strength, biding our time, waiting for the big event."

"Which event is that?"

Kennon smiles.

"Please?"

Kennon says, "You wouldn't understand."

"Try me. And before you say no, remember our pledge of friendship. You can trust me, Kennon. I'm a very good friend to have."

"Very well," she says. "They're coming."

Callie cocks her head. "Who's coming?"

"The Travelers."

Callie pauses. "What is that, a rock band?"

Kennon laughs. "I've said way too much already."

She turns to leave.

Callie says, "Please. Who are the Travelers?"

Kennon pauses a moment, then says, "Ask the child."

"Which child?"

"You'll know her when you see her."

THE END

Personal Message from John Locke:

I LOVE WRITING books! But what I love even more is hearing from readers. If you enjoyed this or any of my other books, it would mean the world to me if you'd send a short email to introduce yourself and say hi. I always personally respond to my readers.

I would also love to put you on my mailing list to receive notifications about future books, updates, and contests.

Let the fun begin here:
http://www.donovancreed.com/Contact.aspx

Or visit my website, http://www.DonovanCreed.com

John Locke

New York Times Best Selling Author
8th Member of the Kindle Million Sales Club
(which includes James Patterson, Stieg Larsson, George R.R. Martin and Lee Child, among others)

John Locke had 4 of the top 10 eBooks on
Amazon/Kindle at the same time, including #1 and #2!

...Had 6 of the top 20, and 8 books in the
top 43 at the same time!

...Has written 25 books in four years in
seven separate genres, all best-sellers!

...Has been published in numerous languages by many of the
world's most prestigious publishing houses!

John Locke

New York Times Best Selling Author
#1 Best Selling Author on Amazon Kindle

Donovan Creed Series:
Lethal People
Lethal Experiment
Saving Rachel
Now & Then
Wish List
A Girl Like You
Vegas Moon
The Love You Crave
Maybe
Callie's Last Dance
Because We Can!

Emmett Love Series:
Follow the Stone
Don't Poke the Bear!
Emmett & Gentry
Goodbye, Enorma

Dani Ripper Series:
Call Me!
Promise You Won't Tell?
Teacher, Teacher

Dr. Gideon Box Series:
Bad Doctor
Box
Outside the Box

Other:
Kill Jill
Casting Call

Young Adult:
A Kiss for Luck (Kindle Only)

Non-Fiction:
How I Sold 1 Million eBooks in 5 Months!